ON IRELAND • CHARLES SILANEY • LEE TAYLOR • CLYDE MARTIN • GEORGE MARTIN • TAD MICHEL
ELMING • DON REED • DAN CHAPMAN • OLAF RODEGARD • LEE ST. JOHN • PEPI GABL • ERIC SAILER
NDALL • KEVIN MURPHY • GREG RETZLAFF • ROY RICHARDSON • DAVE BUTT • MRS. STRAIGHT •
EL WHEELER • ANNA SCHMITT • CHARLIE LAKE • CHARLIE GRAY • CHARLIE SPERR • CHARLIE VAN
E KINNEY DELANEY • ANN WARD JENKINS • ERNST SCHUTZ • KIRK WORRALL • PEGGY ELWOOD •
PH CAULKINS • NORM LILY • DAN WOLF • JUANITA HAGEN • JOHN WOODWARD • HANK SIMONSON
. RILEY & KITTY CATON • KAREN & RAY GILLIAM • WARREN CLANCY • BIG CHRIS • RONI NOLAN •
ON • ERNIE DRAPELA • JOHN & JUDY POWELL • BARBARA PETERSON • DICK KORTZEBORN • JOHN
ERRIS • LILLIAN DUBROKA • JOANN TILTON • SHIRLEY MORGAN • JERRY & KAY GOMES • DEAN &
OHN & SUE VENNER • LARRY SLOAN • DONNA CASSIDY • MIKE & JUDY LOCKHART • JOE CORNELL •
ER • ANNIE GODSEY • BRIAN PERRY • ELMER FAUBIAN • MARCIA ACOSTA • BILL MARONAY • JAN
HAUGK • CHRISTY AEPPLI BUCK • SHELBY AEPPLI HENKEL • RON & ALICE LEWIS • BOB STOLTZ •
KS • DEBBIE KING BROCK • RALPH LEEHAM • TOM KELNER • ADOLF STOCKER • JIM McGUIN • HAL
Y BRITTAN • CARL ZEAMER • FLORIAN & MARY LOU WIPPER • PAULETTE PERRY • MIKE KASTER •
LANCHARD • RICH LITTLE • CAL ANDREWS • JEAN CLAUSING • JOHN WEST • MATT RODE • RICH
. KENT POWLOSKI • GARY HERTZ • KEN KOHNSTAMM • JOHN & DONNA GIRGEN • GLEN VICKERY •
NG BRIXUS • MARGOT CASE • SALLY ANDREWS • DENNIS KEANE • DICK RUGG • TONY WARWICK •
E HATFIELD • SUSAN BOZELL • MICHAEL WESTWOOD • BOB WEST • HANK BENDINELLI • WILLIE
ARY JANE DEVANEY VALIAN • JANE SWIFT • KIM LINDQUIST • GLORIA & DAVID OLSON • LEIF ERIC
GARDNER • BILL & PAM BRETT • SHAWN DOUGHERTY • ARTIE SPEICHER • BECKY TALSMA • STEVE
KOSH & MARLENE PEOPLES • KEN BICKLER • AIDEN THOMPSON • TINA & BOB DONOVAN • JEFF
HNSON • BILL LOHRER • DARRELL & LORI SNOWBARGER • BILL & PEGGY CONERLY • PAM BROWN •
OWER • LINDA REID • GARY HOHNSTEIN • LESLIE SZANTO • JERRY & PAM ASHLAND • CLIF RATH •
NGSTERFER • LINDA ROGERS • TOM JACKSON • JAYNE JOHNSON BROWN • CINDY PERNSTEINER •
ROLYN HODGSON • DENNIS BURMASTER • DALE CROCKATT • DARRELL WINTERBOURNE • LARRY
YOUNG • FACES N' PLACES • THE OREGONIAN • EUGENE REGISTER GUARD • GRESHAM OUTLOOK •
ION LEAGUE OF OREGON • FINNEGAN'S TOY STORE • KATHLEEN COOL • DALE CHIHULY • LAMAR
ER HERO • NANCY LINDBERG • LEVERETT & VIRGINIA RICHARDS • TERRY COCHRAN • VIRGINIA
TAYLOR • GARY MARK • WILLIE REIN • FRED RIGUTTO • MARIO FERRARIN • DICK HOLLENBECK •
RBARA & JACK McCLARTY • HIRSCH-WEISS • LUCILLE KELLY • KESSLER & CO. • CHARLIE KELLER •
McANINICH FAMILY • MR. & MRS. J.J. ADAMSON • LINDA ADAMSON • MR. & MRS. PAUL ALDINGER •
N APPELGREN • EVELYN ARNOLD • MR. & MRS. GERALD AVERY • HAROLD & SHIRLEY BABCOCK •
ROGER BARBER • LOUISE BATES • PETER BEHN • ELSIE BROOKS BELKNAP • PIETRO BELLUSCHI •
ELD • JEFFREY BLANCHFIELD • MR. & MRS. T. BOARDMAN • DORIS SWAYSE BOUNDS • MITCHELL
WN • MR. & MRS. WESLEY BULL • DR. & MRS. OTIS BURRIS • GLENN & IMA BUTTERWORTH • MR. &
RR • MR. & MRS. L.M. CARROLL • JOHN & MARLIS CARSON • ELOISE CARSON LAWRENCE • L. CARYL
OUNTY BANK • BETTY CLEATOR • SHIRLEY COATE • GEORGE COLEMAN • COMBINED FEDERAL
• WALTER CREESE • DAVID CRESSLER • JULIE McCARL • MARSH & BETTY CRONYN • MR. & MRS. J.
DEFENBAUGH • NATALIE DELORD • MARIE DEUELL • MONY DIMITRE • GLADYS DOBSON • DIANE
R. & MRS. DONALD DRAKE • MRS. EDWARD DRAKE • FRANZ DRINKER • D.H. DRYNAN • ELIZABETH
TON • BARBARA ELDRIDGE • FRANCES ELLERY • MARGARET ELLIOT • GLADYS EVERETT • NANCIE
EN FENTON • CURTIS FINCH • WILLIAM & MARILYN FLETCHER • LINN FORREST • GENE FORREST •
L • REKA & FERENC GABOR • WARD & VEE GANO • STUART & SYLVIA GATES • E. CARL • F. GATZKE •
N • MARY GREELEY • JOAN IRWIN GREEN • DOROTHY GREENWOOD • MOLLIE GREGORY • MABEL
YNTHIA HAMANN • LESLIE HARA • SALLY & JIM HARDING • TOM HARDY • MR. & MRS. L.W. HARRIS,
PETER HEITKEMPER • GEORGE HENDERSON • MR. & MRS. ALFRED HERMAN • ORVAL & HELEN
• THE HOFFMAN FUND • MARY HOFFMAN • DR. WILLIAM HOLADAY • JILL HOOPES • JOHN HOPPER
NTINGTON • DR. & MRS. PETER HURST • BILL & BARBARA HUTCHINSON • C. MARLIN ICENOGLE •
AH • MARGE JOHNSON • ROBERT & VIRGINIA JOHNSON • GARY JONES • JERRY JONES • MR. & MRS.
KELLER • LEE KELLY • MARION KELLY • JANE KENDALL • GEORGE KERR • RANDALL & RACHAEL
A KNUTSON • DR. LEW KRAKAUER • LaVERNE KRAUSE • MRS. ELEANOR KRYDER • PAUL & DONNA
CK LENOR LARSEN • WILLIAM & VIRGINIA LAWRENCE • ROBERT LEE • MOSHE & HILDA LENSKE •
RY LINNANE • PHIL & MARGOT LIVESLEY • PAUL LIVINGSTON • JENNY & ROBIN LOCKE • BAYLOR &
ALARKEY • PETE & MARY MARK • SARAH MARK • RUSS & BETTY MAUGANS • JOE McCOY • MR. & MRS.
MEIKIE • CHARLES MERRITT • PHYLLIS MEYER • LIZA MICKLE • L.H. MILBURN • ANDREW MILLAR
UB OF AMERICA, CHARLES BLINCO • LARRY MONTGOMERY • WILLIAM & ROBERTA MORFELD • MR.
R • SARAH & RICHARD MUNRO • LOIS MURPHY • MIDGE NASIATKA • ARTHUR NESTLE • MR. & MRS.
& HATTIE NUDELMAN • GREGORY NYEHOLT • ELIZABETH ODGEN • DR. DAVID OLSON • DAVID
INSTITUTE • EILEEN ORT • MR. & MRS. W. OTTOSON • PHILIP PADELFORD • JAMES PALMER • JOHN
& JEAN PERKINS • MR. & MRS. DONALD PETERSON • MARTHA PHILLIPP • DOROTHY & FRANK
MAN • DAVID POWERS • BETSY PREBLE • SHARR PROHASKA • DAVID & PAT PUGH • ROBERT PUZAS •
EIKE • DOROTHY RICH • MARGE RILEY • MR. & MRS. RICHARD RITZ • JAMES ROBERTS • LOY & ANN
PORTLAND UNIT MOUNTAIN RESCUE • GENNY FRANK • CALDER McCOLL • THOMAS WRIGHTSON

# TIMBERLINE LODGE
## A LOVE STORY

Published Jointly By:

Friends of Timberline and
Graphic Arts Center Publishing Company

Editor-in-Chief & Designer: Judith Rose
Senior Advisor: Douglas Pfeiffer
Editor: Catherine Gleason
Design Consultant: Malcolm Dean
Editorial Consultant: Sarah Munro

International Standard Book Number: 0-932575-24-2
Library of Congress Catalogue Card Number: 86-82136
Graphic Arts Center Publishing Company
P.O. Box 10306, Portland, OR 97210

Photograph pages 4-5: Ray Atkeson—Timberline Lodge in the 1940s.
Photograph pages 8-9: Lawrence Hudetz—Timberline Lodge, fall, 1986.

Dedicated to the many people who have loved
Timberline Lodge during the past fifty years.

# CONTENTS

## BEGINNINGS
### THE UPHILL MOVEMENT    13
by Gideon Bosker

## A DREAM
### THE HOUSE THAT OREGON BUILT    23
by Terence O'Donnell

## THE CHALLENGE
### ONE MAN'S DREAM    47
by Patricia Failing

## A RENAISSANCE
### THE DREAM RENEWED    65
by Jane Van Cleve

## FRIENDS AND LOVERS
### A PERSONAL VIEW    79
by Jack Mills

## EXHILARATION
### ON THE MOUNTAIN    93
by Tom McAllister

## EPILOGUE
### THE LODESTONE    117
by Lute Jerstad

### BIBLIOGRAPHY    126
by Sarah Munro

## ACKNOWLEDGMENTS

I would like to thank the individuals who generously contributed their time and knowledge to this project. I am especially indebted to Douglas Pfeiffer, Michael Hopkins, and Jean Andrews of Graphic Arts Center Publishing Company for their support and advice; to Catherine Gleason for her outstanding job as editor; to Malcolm Dean for his exceptional design and production assistance; to Sarah Munro for editorial consultation; and George M. Henderson of the Independent College Foundation, Dick Hoffmann of the U.S. Forest Service, and Linny Adamson, curator of Timberline Lodge, for historical research.

My appreciation goes to Richard Kohnstamm and Vida Lohnes, Timberline Lodge; John Carson, President, Friends of Timberline; and Robert Ames, Chairman, Fiftieth Anniversary Committee, for their commitment and continuing dedication to Timberline Lodge. —Judith Rose

# TIMBERLINE LODGE

# BEGINNINGS

## THE UPHILL MOVEMENT
### by Gideon Bosker

Proud and glorious with its razor-sharp peak, Mount Hood has been an omnipresent reminder of pioneer values and was held in high esteem by Portland's financial and political elite during the 1920s. By the end of the decade, reverence for the mountain reached new heights. "I am a native son of Oregon. . .and yield to no one in sentimental regard to Mount Hood," wrote John A. Lee, a Mazamas mountaineering club member, in 1927. "It is one of the noblest and most beautiful of our mountains and its historic associations I value highly."

Lee was voicing a deep-seated affection for the mountain shared in the 1920s by many in Portland and particularly by its elite class. This group viewed Mount Hood as a place for spiritual invigoration. They also saw it as an antidote to the urban ills and class tensions which had begun to taint modern city life, even in outposts as remote as Portland. In addition to its role in linking the city's leaders to a romanticized pioneer past, Mount Hood also symbolized vigor and vitality. Arduous conditions on the glacial peak, especially during winter, attracted a hardy breed of mountaineers who recreated on its silky slopes in pursuit of self-sufficiency and adventure. This was a committed, tightly knit retinue of skiers and mountaineering enthusiasts who, declared Richard Montague in a 1920 speech delivered before the Mazamas Club, made the pilgrimage to Mount Hood to feel "the stirrings of ancestral instinct, harking back to the time when these surroundings of hill and heather. . .were the theater of all our joys and sorrows, the scene and setting of human life."

**Page 12:** *To those who know and love it, Mount Hood has symbolized freedom of action, introspection, and aspiration. (Photo: Charlie Borland)*

**Previous Page:** *Owl newel post. (Photo: Tom Iraci)*

**Top:** *The first portal on the Mount Hood Loop Highway near Zig Zag ranger station led the intrepid traveler to Mount Hood. (U.S. Forest Service)*

**Above:** *Skiers from the twenties move toward the site of the yet-to-be-constructed Timberline Lodge as fast as their techniques and equipment allow. (Photo: Ray Atkeson)*

The *Oregon Journal* summarized this collective spirit when it declared that "snow offers the true test for the condition of a man's soul. . . ." By the late 1920s, recreation on the mountain had been elevated to the status of a religion, or, as Portland graphic artist Douglas Lynch put it, "Our theology was the outdoors." Unfortunately, regular excursions to the mountain were restricted for the most part to a group of sports-minded young turks who had enough leisure time to take advantage of the area's natural virtues.

Harold Hirsch, general manager of White Stag Corporation, and Jack Meier of the Meier & Frank Department Store family, were among those Portlanders who learned to downhill ski in the East and who, upon returning to the West, made regular outings to Mount Hood. A typical skiing expedition consisted of a leisurely drive two miles past Rhododendron to a point where the road dead-ended. From here, skiers trekked to a small ranger's cabin at timberline, which was used as a warming hut, and then made a single swooping run down the mountain to their cars.

Recreational activities on the mountain occupied not only members of Portland's genteel, well-monied class but an automobile mechanic, a state policeman, a tree faller, and a number of Scandinavians who were members of the Cascade Ski Club. At the end of the decade, private automobile transportation swept the roads and, not surprisingly, interest in the mountain as a refuge from urban life extended beyond the original cadre of enthusiasts. As greater numbers began to look on Mount Hood as an ideal setting for brief vacations, a public debate began to simmer as to whether — and if so, in what form — recreational facilities on the mountain should be built.

Up to this time, only one small hostelry welcomed mountain visitors. Cloud Cap Inn, which had stood at timberline on the mountain's north slope since 1889, was a charming architectural structure boasting magisterial views of the mountain's craggy summit on one side and the verdant Hood River Valley on the other. But it never really thrived, nor could its eight guest rooms accommodate vast hordes of tourists who now negotiated — with the help of balloon tires on their cars — the Mount Hood Loop Highway constructed in 1925.

After several years of discussion, the debate surrounding the mountain's fate with respect to large-scale development heated into a stiff boil, polarizing community leaders into two distinct factions. One group, the preservationists, warned against the invasion of nature's shrine by "a coarse unenlightened public," while the others touted the virtues of recreational development,

claiming that new facilities on the mountain would signal to those outside the region Portland's aspirations as a major tourist center. These two visions of the mountain proved to be a landmark confrontation that pitted exclusivists against the civic groups who claimed that development of a tourist facility on the glacial behemoth was essential if Portland was to be delivered from regional obscurity. The issues in this battle set the stage for the construction of Timberline Lodge, which would prove that a public project could honor both the lofty sentiments of pioneers and embrace the public's pent-up desire to participate in the mountain's recreational pleasures.

Interestingly, both those who advocated development and those who railed against it were members of that elite class which had colonized the mountain earlier in the decade. Spearheading the preservationist movement, the Mazamas opposed

*The struggle between those in Portland who wanted to preserve the mountain in its pristine form and those who wanted to develop it for recreation began in the twenties. (Photo: Ray Atkeson)*

15

*Alpenglow, a phenomenon caused here by the setting sun, creates rose-colored light on the mountain snow. (Photo: Ron Cronin)*

the creation of what they called "a mechanized mountain" and warned against fostering consumerist attitudes associated with the "hot dog, jazz, Coney Island" type of amusement center. Despite the Mazamas' bitter opposition, a group of Portland businessmen known as the Mount Hood Committee mounted a major campaign supporting the establishment of a tourist facility. In 1927, L.L. Tyler, an influential committee member and a director of the Cascade Development Company, requested a permit from the National Forest Service to build an $800,000 project consisting of a tram and cableway, tourist camp, gas station, and hotel. The plan drew wide support from a number

16

of leading business and civic organizations, including the East Side Businessmen's Club of Portland, The *Oregonian,* and the Oregon State Chamber of Commerce.

Although Tyler's proposal appeared to be on solid ground, District Forester W.B. Greeley denied the request. Aligning himself with the preservationists, Greeley cited his "sentimental regard for the sacredness of Mount Hood" as the primary reason for turning down the broad-based plan. Stunned by the forester's denial, the Mount Hood Committee appealed Greeley's decision to U.S. Secretary of Agriculture W.M. Jardine. This time, Tyler invoked the polemic of his opponents. He argued that modern amenities were necessary on the mountain "so that one's mind may be in a receptive condition to grasp the inspirations and benefits provided by nature."

Realizing his battle would be uphill, Tyler also appealed to the political sensibilities of his foes. He was vocal in his belief that the mountain should anchor a popular attraction that would be open to large numbers of people from all walks of life. But the business leader also showed sympathy for the Mazamas-backed anti-modernists when he suggested that the mountain "is a realm where people would go and come quickly, gaining the benefits and inspiration of lofty views, and then descending very soon to the levels of auto roads which have already been opened to the whole public." To complete his arguments, Tyler invoked time-honored democratic ideals. Claiming the mountain had, for most of its history, been the quasi-private preserve of the well-heeled and wealthy, he argued that his development plan "will serve to take all classes to the summit of one of the most majestic and inspiring peaks of the Western mountain ranges."

By 1929, the government had still not granted the permit. But later that year, U.S. Secretary of Agriculture Jardine was replaced by Arthur M. Hyde. Hyde took a more conciliatory view toward the Mount Hood Committee and granted approval, providing the project was not "designed merely to handle the largest number of people in the most expeditious and mechanical way." Although Tyler's specific proposal was subsequently deemed an unsuitable "profit-making eyesore," and he eventually bowed out of the project for financial reasons, the stage was set for the development of a large-scale tourist facility which welcomed the public and respected the mountain.

Out of the 1920s emerged the manifesto that Oregon's cloud-scraping guardian belonged to *all* the people. History would eventually prove that a lodge created by melding the talents of many individuals could become as powerful a symbol of Oregon's greatness as the mountain itself.

*Pages 18-19: In the nineteenth century, it took three days by carriage to reach the mountain's base from Portland. Now Timberline Lodge is only 75 minutes' drive from Portland. (Photo: Kent Powloski)*

*Page 20: Illumination Rock offers skiers sweeping vistas and a thrilling downhill run. (Photo: Ray Atkeson)*

*Page 21: Early skier on the everlasting snow fields of Eliot Glacier ventures away from its smooth open terrain to view the spectacular crevasses. (Photo: Ray Atkeson)*

# A DREAM

## THE HOUSE THAT OREGON BUILT
### by Terence O'Donnell

In a sense, Timberline Lodge begins architecturally with a sandal in a cave. The cave is at Fort Rock in Central Oregon, and the sandal is thirteen thousand years old. Here is the first evidence of man in Oregon seeking shelter, warmth, and light in the midst of the maelstrom — the pelting rains, the sleet, the whirling snow and howling winds.

From the cave, man went on to build shelter: to wall and roof, first with cedar plank, brush, and bark; then logs, hewn timbers, shakes; next, board-and-batten, shingles, clapboard; finally, concrete, steel, and glass. Timberline Lodge is the culmination and the recapitulation of this long struggle to fashion a shelter in the maelstrom: the stone cave of the Lodge's entrance; the log and hewn timbers of the interior; the vast roof of shakes; the clapboard, shingles, and board-and-batten of the facade; and finally, that great pane of glass over the cave, the beginning and the end of the long evolution juxtaposed, as though the builders in some unconscious, atavistic way had remembered all that had gone before.

The Lodge goes back in another sense as well, back to the mountain and its range, which, for the pioneers coming from the East, was the barrier to Eden. Thus, Mount Hood became a kind of symbol, this mountain which in the end had not defeated them. The nineteenth-century notion of mastering the mountain and, for that matter, nature in general, is quick to be condemned by the urban twentieth century with its view of nature as a playground. It was no playground for the Indians

*Page 22: A carved and weathered ram's head guards Timberline Lodge. (Photo: Bruce Beauchamp)*

*Previous Page: Beaver newel post (Photo: Ron Cronin)*

*Above: Linn Forrest's rendering shows the Lodge near the rim of Salmon River Canyon. The site was moved 900 feet to the west after a survey in May, 1936. (U.S. Forest Service)*

*Right: An architectural elevation of the Lodge's main entrance dates from the thirties. Supervising Forest Service architect W. I. (Tim) Turner was assisted by a host of others: the irrepressible E. J. Griffith, Oregon's WPA administrator; consulting architect Gilbert Stanley Underwood; Linn A. Forrest, who handled design: William D. Smith, structure; Howard Gifford, interior design; Dean Wright, interiors and hardware; Margery Hoffman Smith, furnishings; and A. D. Taylor, landscaping. (Friends of Timberline Lodge)*

who burned the forests to create the valley prairies so they might have sustenance, no playground for the settlers who wrestled the plow and sweated the harvests to get their bread. And for neither Indian nor white was backpacking in the mountains a form of recreation. They saw things differently because their circumstances were different, harshly so. For the pioneers, penetration of the Cascades, the scaling of their highest peak, and the making of a place high on the mountain where man might live meant that mankind had prevailed.

Cloud Cap Inn, built by Oregon pioneers in the closing years of the nineteenth century, is the embryo of Timberline Lodge. Designed by W.A. Whidden and Ian Lewis, who had trained with McKim, Mead and White (the East Coast firm responsible for introducing the shingle style into American architecture), Cloud Cap was based on what the English called the "Rustic Picturesque." But despite its charm, Cloud Cap did not prosper. Then, with the Good Roads Movement of the 1920s and its catchy slogan, "Get Oregon out of the mud," the Inn became more accessible.

As mountain climbing and skiing gained in popularity, a group of Portland businessmen formed the Cascade Development Company to expand or replace the little Inn with a structure more commodious. Two designs were submitted, by distinguished architects A.E. Doyle and Pietro Belluschi, but neither was favored — or perhaps it was simply that the Com-

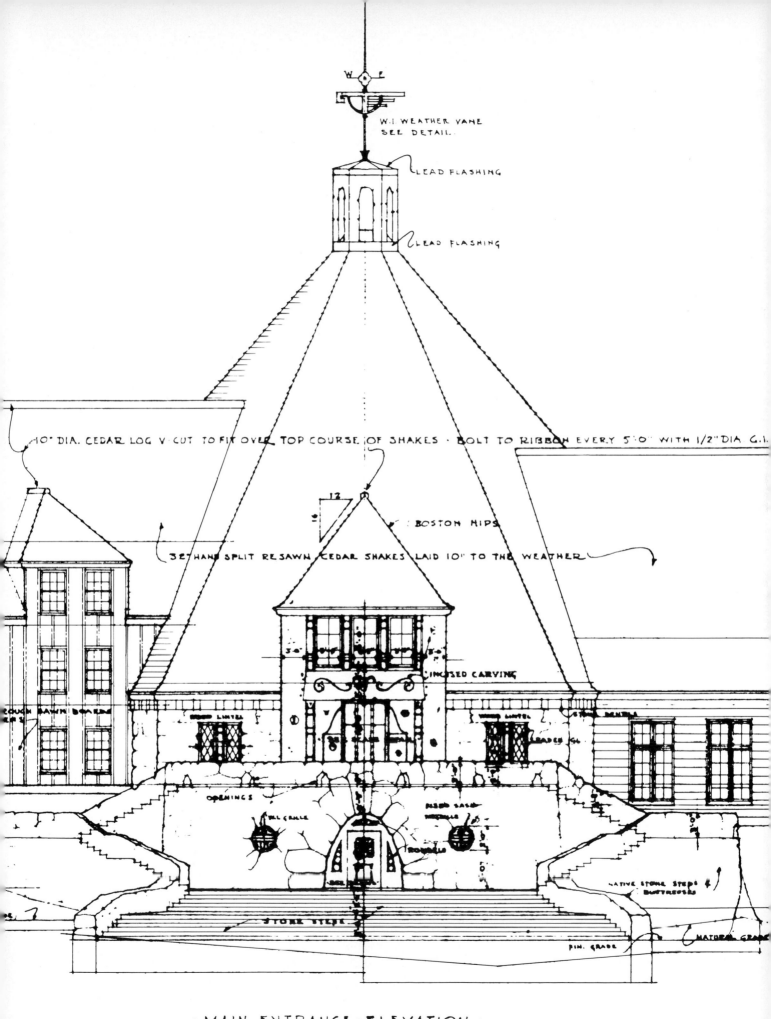

W.I. WEATHER VANE
SEE DETAIL

LEAD FLASHING

LEAD FLASHING

10" DIA. CEDAR LOG V CUT TO FIT OVER TOP COURSE OF SHAKES · BOLT TO RIBBON EVERY 5'0" WITH 1/2" DIA. G.I.

12
16

BOSTON HIPS

32" HAND SPLIT RESAWN CEDAR SHAKES LAID 10" TO THE WEATHER

INCISED CARVING

OPENINGS

NATIVE STONE STEPS &
BUTTRESSES

STONE STEPS

FIN. GRADE

· MAIN · ENTRANCE · ELEVATION ·
SCALE 1/8" = 1'-0"

*Above: The exterior of the Lodge nears completion in the autumn of 1936. It was finished in a relatively short timespan because miraculously little snow fell between September, 1936 and January, 1937. (Oregon Historical Society)*

*Right: Italian masons, who had originally constructed the Columbia River Highway, were put to work building Timberline's stone facade. Four hundred men and women worked on the Lodge; many stayed only two weeks to give others a chance to earn money during the Great Depression. (Photo: George Henderson)*

pany did not have the money to build them. And time passed.

Then, at the beginning of the thirties, the Company submitted another design, this one by Carl Linde, which proposed for the site of the little, snuggled Inn a nine-story glass and concrete skyscraper. This was a departure indeed from the Rustic Picturesque and prompted Frederic Law Olmsted, consultant to the Forest Service, to blast it as "impertinent to the mountain scenery." In 1932, the Company tried again, this time a design by the local architect John Yeon, and again in the modern style, but far more sympathetic to the site than the skyscraper. Still, this design did not meet with Olmsted's approval, and by now the Depression was in full swing and the problem was to maintain what existed rather than to build anew. The project appeared dead.

In 1925, Emerson J. Griffith, a man of remarkable energy, imagination, and persuasiveness, came to live in Portland. At some point Griffith became interested in the moribund hotel project connected with Cloud Cap Inn and with his friend John Yeon brought it back to life. In 1934, Yeon prepared a second

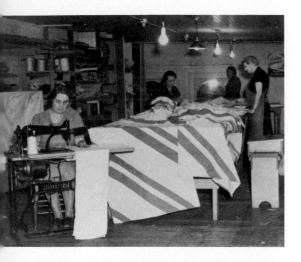

*Top: Over one hundred skilled artisans worked in old public schools in Portland creating handcrafted work for Timberline Lodge. Women made 119 hooked rugs, sewed 100 pairs of appliquéd curtains, and wove 912 yards of drapery and furniture fabric. (Oregon Historical Society)*

*Above: Ironworker Orion B. Dawson stands proudly in front of his Cascade Dining Room gates, which were based on Indian motifs and collaboratively designed by Lodge architect Dean Wright and Margery Hoffman Smith. The Lodge's iron work (181 pieces were originally created) has been called among the finest in the nation. (Friends of Timberline)*

design, which, though still in the modern idiom, was distinctly different from his first. One reason lay in the fact that the site for the Lodge had now been changed.

Skiing on Mount Hood had become increasingly popular in the 1930s due in large part to the promotions of the Portland Winter Sports Association: Harold Hirsch's White Stag fashion shows, winter festivals, and skiing competitions. Frequently, several thousand spectators were in attendance but they went to Government Camp, not Cloud Cap, because the former offered better slopes and was closer to Portland. Government Camp, however, presented problems: accommodations were limited and it was a little distant from the best slopes. For these reasons, Griffith and Yeon chose a site at the timberline, 2,200 feet above Government Camp, in the midst of good slopes, with magnificent vistas of the mountain and surrounding terrain.

The difficulty, which seemed impassable, was to find backers. It was, after all, the Depression. Then, as might be expected in this tale of the Lodge, the unexpected happened. Griffith, who had contacts in the Democratic party, was appointed Director of the Works Progress Administration in Oregon — and that meant money.

Now the Mount Hood Development Association, which Berger Underdahl and the energetic Jack Meier had recently organized, along with Charles Dierli, Franz Drinker, Dr. Paul Dutton, George W. Joseph, L.B. Macnab, E.B. MacNaughton, Walter W.R. May, James A. Mount, Fred Stadter, and Harold F. Wendel, backed the project. Furthermore, and most important, the Forest Service granted use of the land at timberline and agreed to act as sponsors. Griffith, always light on his feet, acted with dispatch and brevity, quickly sending off an application of just one typewritten page requesting a grant of a quarter of a million dollars. The project so pithily proposed promised employment for a variety of people, including artists, on the relief rolls. It provided for public recreation. It assured a measure of scenic preservation. And finally, in the words of historian Dr. Jean Burwell Weir, it would be "a large, highly visible work relief project in Republican Oregon." Harry Hopkins, the WPA's national director, was delighted. In December, 1935, the application was approved.

But of course there were problems. Griffith and the Development Association wanted John Yeon as architect. Washington objected. This was a public project, but Yeon was closely associated with the private development corporation. The Oregon chapter of the American Institute of Architects agreed that the architect should be chosen by public competition, then

almost immediately reversed itself and suggested that the United States Forest Service provide an architect. The Forest Service demurred: its staff architects were versed in designing outhouses, sheds, and shelters, but little else.

Who then was to be the architect, and was the Lodge to be Rustic Picturesque or modern glass and steel? Washington, fed up, thought it had settled the matter by appointing as chief architect Gilbert Stanley Underwood, known for his rustic lodges in several national parks. Washington was wrong. To the surprise of all, the local Forest Service, which had earlier claimed expertise in nothing more than the most basic shelters, entered the arena with architects of its own. The Forest Service named Tim Turner as chief architect, assisted by Howard L. Gifford, Emmett Blanchfield, Linn A. Forrest, Dean Wright, and supervising structural engineer William D. Smith. Turner had definite ideas of

*Oregon women, working for the WPA, fashion the Lodge's spun copper ashtrays. (Oregon Historical Society)*

*Above: Just completed, the interior of the head house or main lobby seems to glow with anticipation. Workers under the supervision of cabinetmaker Ray Neufer created all of the Lodge's 820 pieces of furniture. (Oregon Historical Society)*

*Right: A mountain retreat that nestles above a great wilderness, Timberline Lodge was formally dedicated a National Historic Landmark in 1978. (Photo: Richard Kohnstamm)*

what the Lodge should look like. They were not the same as Underwood's.

Underwood, still under the impression that he was chief architect, prepared a plan very much in the rustic tradition. "One note which must be kept out at all costs," he wrote, "is sophistication." The feature of his plan most at variance with the Lodge as finally built was that the central structure and flanking wings faced the mountain — and the wind.

Turner, meanwhile, was designing *his* Lodge *with* an element of sophistication, taking for his model what Dr. Weir calls the "stately picturesque" style of Northwest estate and country club architecture. His major departure from Underwood's scheme was to turn the Lodge around. He realized from his familiarity with the site that the building should have its back to the wind and the snow drifts that wind would bring.

To complicate these differences, there now entered upon the scene yet a third architect, E.J. Griffith himself. Responsible in part for the idea of the Lodge, and for the WPA allocation, he felt justified in interjecting some design features of his own. "In

every sense of the word,'' writes Dr. Weir, "Timberline Lodge was the product of collaboration, and a collaboration fraught with conflict and competition.''

The conflict dragged on to be settled finally by nature itself. Spring was coming. If construction was to start at this six-thousand-foot site, it would have to start soon. Accordingly, the principals resolved their differences, the final plans were drawn, and on June 13, 1936, construction began — at last.

But how was the Lodge to be decorated and appointed, and from where was the money to come? The resourceful Griffith tackled these problems by calling on that redoubtable Oregon figure, Dr. Burt Brown Barker, educator, scholar, preservationist, and at the time regional director of the Federal Arts Project. Dr. Barker lent his august support and sent off a request for funds to Holger Cahill, the FAP director in Washington. As usual, there were complications.

Cahill adamantly favored the fine arts for his projects — painting, sculpture, and murals in particular. But Griffith, Barker, and the Forest Service architects had decided that for the

Lodge the craft arts of blacksmithing, cabinetmaking, wood carving, and weaving would be more suitable. Cahill was not convinced and turned the project down. Griffith and Barker refused to leave the field without a second attack, and Cahill finally agreed to provide ten thousand dollars. Their plans for the interior now legitimized, Griffith hired Orion B. Dawson, a blacksmith, and Ray Neufer, a cabinetmaker, to supervise the creation of the Lodge's wrought iron and wooden appointments. Also, since it had been suggested by someone that a "woman's touch" was needed, Griffith hired on a temporary basis a local decorator named Margery Hoffman Smith. This "temporary" appointment and its results turned out to be very lasting indeed.

Meanwhile, the Lodge was abuilding. A tent camp for the workers was put up at Summit Meadows, seven miles below the Lodge site. The men — sometimes as many as 150 — were paid ninety cents an hour plus tent and board. All but 10 percent were drawn from the relief rolls, and the crews changed every two weeks to provide employment for more men.

The workers were transported every morning up the mountain in open trucks, preceded by a snowplow. First they dug the excavations, then they built the forms and poured concrete. Stone was brought up on sleds from a nearby quarry, and the masons began the facing of the concrete walls.

The wings completed, it was time by late July to begin construction of the head house, as the six-sided central structure between the wings was called. Here too stone was used: for the entry, for the ground-floor walls and arches, and for the central chimney's massive stack. From the chimney's hub, giant timbers spoked out as rafters to the sides of the hexagon and the arches of grey stone and yellow wood. No area of the Lodge gives a better sense of shelter and safety than this beautifully proportioned room of stone and timber, fires burning at its center.

Construction of the main lounge differed dramatically from the ground floor, for here space was meant to soar like the mountain itself. The instruments of this thrust were six forty-foot shafts of old-growth pine set into the angles of the hexagon. Great struts against the gale-force winds, they were a massive fuselage around which the whole building with its wings gathered for support. After these struts were shaped and finished with axe and adze by Henry Steiner, raised with a gin pole and put in place, Timberline Lodge was up.

Still, there remained much to do. And winter was coming. Fresh funds from Washington, however, were not. While Griffith finagled unsympathetic WPA officials, one of whom

**Previous Page:** *Based on an Indian motif taken from a Camp Fire Girls' handbook, the Lodge's weather vane symbolizes Timberline's Fiftieth Anniversary. Cast in bronze, the 750-pound weather vane was hoisted into place by workers during a blizzard. (U.S. Forest Service)*

**Left:** *Timberline's head house soars like the peak of the mountain itself. The linen-covered chandeliers were fashioned under the supervision of Fred C. Baker, Portland's most prominent light fixture manufacturer. The extraordinary wood finishes were under the supervision of James Duncan. (Photo: Bruce Beauchamp)*

37

*Top:* The iron door of a bread-warming oven was built into the Cascade Dining Room fireplace. (Photo: Ron Cronin)

*Above:* Door latches reminiscent of medieval-style iron work decorate the connecting doors between guest rooms. Friends of Timberline work hard to provide the funds and the energy which lovingly maintain all of Timberline's handcrafted treasures. (Photo: Ron Cronin)

called the Lodge "a lousy project," the workers rushed on: laying the oak-plank flooring, raising the great chimney, constructing the post-and-lintel arches. A keynote of the Lodge and a note struck at the very beginning in the stone entryway, the arches evoked the curving shelter of the primeval cave.

The arches in place, the workers built the ambulatory or mezzanine circling above the main lounge and fitted into its sides wide-windowed bays from which to view the mountains. Finally, they erected the triangular roof supports, extending them horizontally from the tops of the forty-foot shafts to rest on a lip of the stone stack, their angle carried up to brace the spoked rafters of the ceiling.

Racing against the calendar, they next completed the dining room, its curved posts and low, beamed ceiling creating a room reminiscent of the saloon of a great sailing ship. And then they turned to the guest rooms paneled in knotty pine. No one has described their charm and snugness, caught their essence more succinctly than Kary King, a chambermaid at the Lodge, who said, "They're cabiny."

Finally, the stone chimney stack completed, it was time to crown the Lodge. Tim Turner designed the crown — a weather vane cast in bronze — using an Indian motif which suggests a feathered half-moon. Installing the vane was a trick, for it weighed nearly half a ton, and in the midst of placing it atop the chimney stack a blizzard blew up. For winter now had come.

Somewhat earlier in the year, in September, WPA chief Harry Hopkins and an entourage of thirty-five arrived to inspect the Lodge. He and Griffith threw snowballs at one another, toured the building, and finally got down to business — which was money. There was still much to do, particularly in the decoration and appointment of the Lodge, but no money left: the original ten thousand was long since spent. Hopkins, much impressed by what had been done, opened the purse and out came forty thousand dollars. Margery Hoffman Smith got to work.

Mrs. Smith belonged to a family of designers and builders. Her father, Lee Hoffman, constructed Portland's first bridge across the Willamette. Her mother, Julia, designed what is still Portland's most distinguished apartment building and was a national leader in the arts and crafts movement. Mrs. Smith herself, after attending Bryn Mawr and the Art Students League of New York, returned to Portland to set up shop as a decorator. Recommended by John Yeon, she had begun work at Timberline as a "temporary" consultant. Now she was permanent and took over entirely the job at hand.

It was a big job, for Mrs. Smith was to supervise the design

and execution of a vast multiplicity of objects: furniture for the public rooms and forty-eight guest rooms plus all the wood carving; woven curtains, bedspreads, upholstery, and rugs; iron lamps, andirons, smoking stands, gates and grills, and all manner of hardware. Mrs. Smith was also associated with work in parchment, rawhide, paper, canvas, linoleum, and glass. It was a challenge, to say the least, but Mrs. Smith's qualifications were considerable. She was a woman of vigor and decision and thoroughly experienced in problems of design and execution.

The construction of furniture was perhaps Mrs. Smith's biggest job, for over eight hundred individual pieces were required. And there were constraints. The furniture had to be done quickly and had to be exceptionally sturdy. Most daunting of all, the men who were to make the pieces were unskilled in the complex craft of furniture construction and had to be instructed in the task. Fortunately, Mrs. Smith had the expert assistance of Ray Neufer, and the results were both timely and sturdy. The grace of the furniture design is open to question, but one happy device was the shaping of the main lounge sofas as half hexagons. This, together with the log balustrades marking off the fireside areas,

*Top: Paul Bunyan shines in the glass mosaic by Virginia Darcé for the Blue Ox Bar. (Photo: Tom Iraci)*

*Above: The Blue Ox Bar was a bottle club during the late forties, before liquor by the drink was legalized in Oregon. (Photo: Ron Cronin)*

provided for an intimacy of grouping important in a space so vast as the central lounge.

Another aspect of the woodworking project was carving. Abstract Indian designs were carved into the lintels of a number of arches, and several chandeliers were worked in the form of oxbows. (All of Timberline's Indian symbols were copied from a Camp Fire Girls' manual.) The most successful and certainly the most popular of the wood carvings were the twenty-four stairway newel posts in the form of animal figures, now softened and oiled by thousands of hands which over the years have stroked them with affection. In wood, as in other materials, Mrs. Smith carried out her three central motifs: the natural life of the region and its Indian and pioneer heritage.

Creating textiles for the Lodge was also a major undertaking—in the end, nearly a thousand yards of fabric were woven on hand looms. Here Mrs. Smith had the expert assistance of Gladys Everett, Oregon Director of the WPA Women's and Professional Projects. But again, she was faced with largely untrained workers, so simple and quickly teachable designs were in order.

Some of the women who had worked under Miss Everett sewing clothes for needy families were switched to the Timberline project and were taught to weave, appliqué, and hook rugs. Scraps of material from the needy family project were used in the appliqué of curtains, while old Civilian Conservation Corps uniforms and blankets were cut up for the rugs. This was one of the few instances in the whole Timberline project in which a measure of economy was exercised.

Fabrics were used throughout the Lodge, but it was in the guest rooms that they were employed most strikingly. For the forty-eight rooms, twenty-three different motifs were chosen — Monkshood, Bachelor Button, Shooting Star, Solomon Seal, Blue Spruce, to name a few — and coordinated in each room's curtains, rugs, and bedspreads. Mrs. Smith also secured the talents of several artists, including Karl Fuerer, whom Mrs. Smith found living in a piano box, to create watercolors and lithographs of the motifs.

For the wrought iron, lucky Mrs. Smith again had superb assistance, this time in the blacksmith O.B. Dawson. Dawson was no horseshoer under some spreading fir. In his travels he had studied the wrought-iron work of the great European masters and had learned much from Samuel Yellin, a Philadelphian who had gated a number of very grand East Coast estates.

Under Dawson's supervision and with design suggestions from Mrs. Smith and assistant architect Dean Wright, nearly two hundred pieces were fashioned, everything from the simple

straps binding beams together to door latches, knockers, lighting fixtures, andirons (made in some cases from railroad rails), grills, pokers, drapery rods and, in a culminating triumph, the great pinecone-hinged coyote gate of the dining room. The wrought iron at Timberline is among the finest in the nation.

Appropriately, the decoration and appointment of Timberline Lodge was done in the crafts tradition, but Mrs. Smith did not entirely ignore the fine arts. While she worked with Virginia Darcé to create the vivid, sparkling glass mosaics in the Blue Ox bar, she commissioned paintings from some of the Northwest's finest artists: Darrel Austin, Charles Heaney, C.S. Price, and Howard Sewall. She also commissioned Douglas Lynch's incised linoleum murals, which hang in the present auditorium and charmingly portray the region's seasonal recreation. Mrs. Smith covered all bases and there were lots of them.

In general, her achievements were remarkable, both in manner and result: her talents as a designer, her talents as an expediter saw a vast array of striking appointments filling the Lodge in hardly more than a year. Two other aspects of her achievement are best described by Dr. Weir: "her desire to coor-

*Timberline's main stairway is embellished with newel posts designed by Florence Thomas and hand-carved in the shapes of animals and birds from cedar utility posts. Thousands of affectionate hands have polished the newel posts to a high gleam. (Photo: Ron Cronin)*

41

dinate and integrate her work with that of the architects," which is a rare accomplishment, and rarer still her ability to provide "a coherent, unified statement of aesthetic goals."

At some point in 1937 Griffith heard that President Franklin Roosevelt would visit Oregon to dedicate Bonneville Dam. Working through Oregon Congresswoman Nan Wood Honeyman, a friend of the Roosevelts, Griffith strongly urged the President to dedicate the Lodge as well or, better yet, and with colossal insouciance on Griffith's part, that the President dispense with Bonneville and dedicate the Lodge alone. Griffith knew that a presidential dedication would provide the ultimate in recognition and, quite as important if not more so, would loosen the WPA's purse strings, for once again the Lodge had far exceeded its budget.

The Roosevelts were not enthusiastic. Bonneville, they felt, was enough for one day and a dedication at Timberline would mean a sixty-mile detour for the weary presidential party en route from the dam to Portland. But Griffith, as was his way, prevailed.

Griffith had assured Washington that the Lodge was ready for the presidential visit, a statement true insofar as structure was concerned but patently false as regards the interior. However, with the lever of the visit Griffith obtained more funds to hire more workers and in the nick of time the Fish and Brook guest room was completed for the President, the Solomon Seal room was prepared for Mrs. Roosevelt, and fourteen other rooms were ready for their staff.

On the morning of September 28, the President, his lady, and an entourage of ninety arrived at the Lodge to be greeted by an assemblage of twelve hundred. At 1:30 P.M., the President stood on the terrace above the entrance and delivered his fifteen-minute dedication. He hardly mentioned the Lodge but dwelt instead on the Oregon economy, the usefulness of the Forest Service, and the importance of public recreation.

The true dedication of Timberline Lodge occurred a few

*The catalogued treasures of Timberline Lodge number well over three hundred works and include a hand-painted botanical from a project on which Dora Erickson, Karl Feurer, and Martina Gangle worked, and a watercolor by E.A. Lewandowski. (Photos: Don Condit)*

months later and it is described by E.J. Griffith:

> *When the job was finished the first group to hold a banquet in the lodge's magnificent dining room was the thirty odd superintendents and foremen who had bossed the construction.... They were rough men and they had met to eat and drink and celebrate a job of which they were intensely proud. It was a mid-winter night with the snow piled thirty feet deep against the windows. But the banquet did not go off with the jollity that had been planned. As each man was called on to speak, he bid a faltering farewell to beams that had been shaped with loving hands — to a job that had put new hope into many hearts. Eyes glistened as they organized Timberline Guild and pledged themselves to meet each year at Timberline Lodge to drink a toast to a job well done.*

For Timberline Lodge was more than just a building.

There are few left who remember the Great Depression. Excepting the Civil War, it was the most devastating experience through which the nation has ever passed: desperate men, frightened women, hungry children, millions of them. The Lodge provided work in the plain, material sense of the word for some of them. But it also provided something over and above the ninety cents an hour, the heated tent, the three good meals. It provided the pride and purpose without which men and women will also starve. For this was the great injury the Depression did, not so much to the body of the nation as to its spirit.

In a secular sense, the spirit which built the Lodge is analogous to the spirit which built the great cathedrals: men and women working together to build something strong and beautiful which would express and celebrate their place. It is a spirit which still pervades the Lodge. Another chambermaid, Kathy "Peachy" Keen, turning at the door of a guest room as she was about to leave, said something which was meant for today but which applies to the past as well. "There's a lot of work," she said, pausing to touch the gleaming panel of the door, "but there's also a lot of pride."

So stands the Lodge which pride and purpose built. In its exterior it expresses a quality few buildings possess: it *belongs* to its place. In part this lies in the wood and stone of its material, in part in the design of those hip-roofed wings sloping down to tie it to the earth. The Lodge gives this sense of belonging in another

way by subtly prefiguring what lies behind it: the wings like the mountain's ramparts, the head house rising above all like the mountain peak itself. It is difficult to imagine another building in its place.

Nor is it easy to imagine that it should have another interior. Here the central quality is its woodenness and the powerful sense of interlocking structure which these wooden elements impart. Most buildings give the impression of having been assembled; the Lodge in the most tactile of ways gives the impression of having been built. And though the old building creaks in the onslaught of one-hundred-mile gale winds and snow drifts of thirty feet, yet it stands firm, there at the center of the maelstrom.

*Part of Erich Lamade's carved wood relief above the Cascade Dining Room fireplace shows an Oregon bear and several stylized birds. (Photo: Don Condit)*

45

# THE CHALLENGE

## ONE MAN'S VISION
### by Patricia Failing

Timberline historians are unanimous in concluding that the Lodge reached a fortuitous turning point in 1955. In that year Richard Kohnstamm, a twenty-nine-year-old former social worker with no experience in lodge management, became operator of then-bankrupt Timberline Lodge. To date, Kohnstamm has directed Timberline's development for thirty-one of its fifty years, confirming an early prediction that he would succeed because he did not know how to fail.

Hotel-business veterans of the early 1950s were of the opinion that "only a crazy man or a millionaire" would take on Timberline Lodge. Neither description exactly fits Kohnstamm, although he is a member of a prosperous family of food color manufacturers and he does profess to be in love with the fifty-year-old Lodge. Both factors have proven essential in his tenure as operator and helped secure his position as impresario of Timberline's renaissance. His master's degree in social work from Columbia University also proved essential in dealing with scores of workers and hundreds of guests who come together every day to form, in effect, a small Mount Hood community.

Kohnstamm stresses that no single individual can be credited with the successful operation of Timberline Lodge. "This place really runs on the devotion of the many, many people who work here," he points out. "They are not doing it just for the bucks. Imagine, week after week, digging your car out of the snow to go to work, working eight hours, and then digging out your car to go home. Imagine digging out the old Magic Mile

*Page 46:* Richard Kohnstamm took
over the Lodge operations in 1955.
Although its only chairlift was
broken and the Lodge itself lay close
to ruin, work by Kohnstamm and
many others have restored the
historic Lodge. (Photo: Jeff Becker)

*Previous Page:* Eagle newel post
(Photo: Richard Kohnstamm)

*Above:* Rolf Achtel works the
controls of the first portable lift on
the upper reaches of Mount Hood in
1959. (Photo: Richard Kohnstamm)

*Right Top:* Employees Molly
DeLong (Kohnstamm) and Ron
Lewis use the Palmer lift's
predecessor, which handled just six
people at a time but represented the
humble beginnings of the largest
summer ski operation in North
America. (Photo: Richard
Kohnstamm)

chairlift by hand, which is what we had to do in the early days.
Think about spending all day plowing out the parking lot and
then having it snow four feet that night. That's what it's like to
work here and yet we've had employees willing to live in their
cars or hike half a mile through unplowed snow to bunk in a
cabin just so they could work at Timberline. It's not just the arts
and crafts at the Lodge that represent personal dedication. So
does almost every mundane aspect of daily operation, as long-
time employees like Carol Haugk will tell you. There's a *lot* of
romanticism here.''

Working conditions at Timberline helped defeat a series of
less romantic and undercapitalized operators in the early 1950s.
In the winter of 1954-55, the Lodge was shut down for non-
payment of utility bills and padlocked by the Internal Revenue
Service. Just prior to the shutdown gambling and prostitution
found their way into the Lodge.

Timberline's nadir, however, was preceded by a period of
prosperity. Prior to 1952, Lodge operations were overseen by
Timberline Lodge, Incorporated, an organization of Portland
businessmen. Founding members included Forrest Berg, Robert

Burns, Ambrose Cronin Sr., William Healey Sr., Horace Mecklem Sr., Jack Meier, and Fred Van Dyke.

Under the direction of the Corporation, the Lodge essentially paid its own way. By the late 1940s as many as five thousand skiers crowded the slopes on a typical weekend. Long lines formed for the three rope tows and Magic Mile chairlift, and the Silcox Hut at the top of the Magic Mile dispensed volumes of refreshments. Demand was high for dormitory bunks, which could be had for $2.50 a night, as well as for the Lodge's private rooms. Timberline's operation eventually became so time-consuming that the Corporation decided to turn the business over to a resident private operator. None was able to maintain the organization's record of success, and the Lodge entered its period of decline.

Fascinated by the site, weekend skier Kohnstamm decided that he could restore Timberline's fortunes. When he took over the property, he expected the Lodge would need renovation and repair. He was appalled, however, to discover the full extent of the deterioration. Hand-woven draperies had been stuffed in broken windowpanes and hand-made furniture used for fire-wood. Costs for repairing scarred woodwork alone ran $15,000 per room. More than a thousand fire-code violations needed correcting. The only chairlift was in shambles.

In December, 1955, Kohnstamm reopened Timberline with the new $100,000 Pucci chairlift. Located on sheltered slopes below the Lodge, the Pucci lift could operate when drifts and storms shut down the Magic Mile. *Sports Illustrated* reported that "after a miracle of restoration. . . the skiers are back and the future is bright." Weekend crowds quickly grew and Kohn-stamm began to envision a new gondola opening Mount Hood's perpetual snowfields to summer skiers. Between 1955 and 1966, RLK Company, the family concern Kohnstamm estab-lished to operate the Lodge, invested more than a half-million dollars in Timberline, repairing the building, installing a heated swimming pool and the Pucci and Victoria Station chairlifts, and acquiring Sno-Cats to transport skiers and tourists.

Meanwhile, Kohnstamm was learning that "nothing comes simply at Timberline — *nothing*. The Lodge didn't have a load-ing dock, so every crate of lettuce had to be manhandled into the building and put into a little dumbwaiter that served the kitchen. The attic was up a narrow, winding staircase and there's no place else to store furniture if you decide to change the configu-ration of a room. We had a rinky-dink Ford engine that ran the water pump for the Lodge and it would hardly make it through the night without breaking down. We had to ask lift-crew guys

*Sno-Cats were provided for skiers and tourists from 1955 to 1978. (Oregon Economic Development Department)*

49

*Left: All too often, the Magic Mile's cable iced and crashed down, causing more work for crews struggling to dig out the chairs buried by storms. The new Magic Mile was built by the Oregon and California (O & C) Counties Association thanks to the help of Darrell Jones and George Henderson. (Photo: Ray Atkeson)*

*Page 52: This unusual aerial view shows the Lodge in 1974 cut off from the outside world, its road snowed in. It was three days before the road reopened — the longest time Timberline has been cut off in thirty-five years. (Photo: Alden Hugh)*

to sleep in this oil-soaked, gas-soaked little pumphouse in case it quit. The winters were especially heavy in the early years. Our road was always a mess and it was a real adventure just to get the mail. It was *very* slow going at first, like trying to push a locomotive off dead center.''

The ski boom and back-to-nature sentiments of the 1960s brought new momentum to Timberline and strengthened its economic base. The Lodge also grew in status as a tourist attraction, drawing 750,000 visitors annually by 1969. But the wages of this popularity were severe: thousands of tourists were literally wearing away the historic building. Eighty percent were sightseers who spent fifty cents or less while visiting.

Kohnstamm and the United States Forest Service, the governmental agency with jurisdiction over the Lodge, developed plans for new facilities to accommodate the burgeoning crowds. But the Forest Service, lacking the funding to implement the plan, told Kohnstamm that finding the money was his responsibility. In 1969 Kohnstamm took his case to Washington, testifying on Timberline's behalf before the House and Senate appropriation committees. The first problem he faced

*Members of the* Lost Horizon *crew, which starred Liv Ullman, Michael York, Peter Finch, and Olivia Hussey, used the Lodge as a base during the movie's 1973 filming. The crew used a helicopter to create blizzard conditions. The rickety Tibetan bridge was filmed in the parking lot. (Photos: Richard Kohnstamm)*

53

was describing Timberline — a ski resort that is primarily an architectural monument and tourist attraction. In his testimony he stressed the urgent need for construction of a day lodge "to take the great burden of recreational masses out of Timberline, which is essentially a hotel and, believe it or not, a museum." Running Timberline without a day lodge, he told the congressional committees, "is like trying to run an exclusive restaurant in the Lincoln Memorial."

In addition to the day lodge, Kohnstamm lobbied for funds to complete Timberline's original design, which included an east wing convention center. Monies were appropriated in the early 1970s to complete a maintenance building and the convention wing, but these allocations were not made by the Forest Service. At the urging of the Oregon congressional delegation, supplementary funds were added to pre-existing Forest Service budgets to finance the new construction.

During these years, Kohnstamm's personal debates with the Forest Service intensified. Timberline is located in a National Forest, which is governed by the Forest Service. The agency leases the resort to a private operator for an annual sum; the operator, in turn, may add revenue-enhancing facilities to the property. In light of Timberline's evident rejuvenation, the Forest Service decreed that Kohnstamm's lease fees would be quadrupled. After four years of negotiation by Timberline attorney Norm Wiener and the intervention of United States Senators Bob Packwood and Mark Hatfield, agreement on a new thirty-year operating permit was finally reached. Wright Mallery, supervisor of Mount Hood National Forest, explained that "throughout the negotiations we had Kohnstamm in mind as the man most devoted to the mountain and best able to offer the kind of service the Lodge deserves. The problem was how to accommodate a national fee structure to a unique facility like Timberline Lodge."

In Kohnstamm's estimation, RLK Company came of age during these negotiations. "We learned that we have to see our situation in a broader context. There's rivalry over the allocation of funds and mixed feelings about priorities within the Forest Service itself. Part of the Forest Service looks upon itself as

*Above: Timberline's pool, which was built in 1959, is now complemented by an 18-seat outdoor hot tub. (Photo: Richard Kohnstamm)*

*Above Center: A rare shot of the geothermal well which gushes upward from the bottom of Pucci's Glade. Water temperatures of 211 degrees Fahrenheit have been recorded at the site, whose discovery was a cooperative venture between RLK & Company and the State of Oregon under the supervision of geologist Dick Bowen. (Photo: Richard Kohnstamm)*

*Above Right: From time to time, new Saint Bernard puppies are brought to begin pampered careers as Timberline Lodge mascots. (Photo: Lawrence Hudetz)*

*Right: Bruno and Heidi take a beneficent view of the world. Saint Bernards are a tradition which began almost as soon as the Lodge was dedicated. They continue to be one of Timberline's most popular attractions. (Photo: Molly Kohnstamm)*

guardian of the forest and seems to think all entrepreneurs are coming to rape the forest, exploit the people, make a ton of money, and run away to Mexico. There are others in the service who know that we do need places like Timberline where people can easily associate with the out-of-doors.

"There are difficult philosophical questions involved here," he continues. "What's the proper balance between preservation and recreation? Who does Timberline really belong to? What is its true identity? Our debates with the Forest Service should be seen from this perspective. Things have gradually improved between us and now they are getting on the bandwagon. My goal is to push things further, to create a climate of enthusiasm that will encourage the Forest Service to become a dynamic force for Timberline's success. They should be *proud* of Timberline and I think that's beginning to happen."

In 1972, construction began on Timberline's east wing convention center, due to lobbying efforts by Oregon Congressmen Bob Duncan and Al Ullman. As the interior was being finished in 1974, the Lodge was buried under the heaviest snowfall ever recorded on Mount Hood. The fire sprinkler system in the new addition froze. The corridor connecting the wing to the Lodge partially collapsed under the weight of the snow. An ice pack formed on the roof and tore the wing away from the main building. "This kind of experience gives you such a respect for conditions on Mount Hood," Timberline engineer Walt Aeppli observes. "Most of the time you look at Timberline Lodge and think it's overbuilt, that it's done for style and effect. But in years like 1974 the building needed all the strength it had to withstand thirty feet of snow.."

Informally christened "the C.S. Price wing" in honor of Oregon's early abstract painter, whose work hangs in the lobby, the convention center was completed in 1975. The next major

expansion of Timberline's facilities, the Palmer chairlift, had been in Kohnstamm's mind since 1955. Financing for the lift, which provided the first summer skiing in North America, was arranged in the early 1970s, but commitments fell apart under protracted negotiations for renewal of the operating permit. After the renewal, a local bank agreed to provide funding, but the agreement collapsed when Timberline's revenues were undermined by severe drought conditions in 1976.

To raise the necessary capital, Kohnstamm conceived what he regards as his most creative financial strategy: the 2000 Club. In 1976 he offered skiers a package of lift tickets for $2,000 that would entitle them to use all of Timberline's lifts until the year 2000. Buyers snapped up the proposition and Kohnstamm quickly raised the $300,000 necessary to begin construction.

Financing was but one of the obstacles to completion of the Palmer chairlift. Others were environmental and philosophical. Many mountain climbers regarded the lift as an offensive commercial intrusion and contested Kohnstamm's right to erect the structure on Mount Hood's perpetual snowfields. After numerous environmental studies and heated debate, permission was finally granted in 1977 to install the lift at the 8,500-foot level. A physical battle ensued: three towers blew down the first winter, and some industry observers predicted the lift would never run.

The prediction proved incorrect, thanks in large measure to the expertise of Timberline's Hill Manager Steve Haugk and his assistant Bill Brett. With Palmer attracting more than 30,000 skiers each summer, Timberline is now an economically viable year-round resort, drawing summer business that has also begun to revitalize nearby Government Camp.

The much-needed day lodge was opened in 1981, and Kohnstamm credits former Congressman Wendell Wyatt with nailing down the necessary congressional appropriation. "In a real sense it's his day lodge," says Kohnstamm. "Sometimes it's hard to appreciate politicians, but Timberline could never have made progress without them."

Confirming Kohnstamm's view that nothing comes simply at Timberline, the first designs for the day lodge proved unacceptable and new architects had to be found. The question of physical and architectural compatibility between the old building and the new lodge proved especially difficult to resolve. Environmental realities, including thirty-foot snowdrifts and eighty-knot winds, further complicated the design process. Construction of the $7.2 million facility finally began in 1978. By then Timberline was being engulfed by nearly one million visitors a year.

"I was absolutely determined that all these developments would happen," Kohnstamm says. "But the process was exhausting. I kept feeling as though I was pushing the Forest Service ahead of me with one hand and then tugging Timberline behind me with the other to make things progress and improve. This is why Friends of Timberline [established in 1975] has been so important to me personally. What I really appreciate is the feeling of strength and cooperation that comes from this group of people saying, 'Hey — we're here to help, period.' Of course they were essentially here to restore Timberline's artwork, but it was *help*."

*Left Top: Mountain High festivals are sponsored every other year by Friends of Timberline. At the 1983 festival, glass artist Paul Marioni, who created a glass mural for the day lodge, was honored. (Photo: Richard Kohnstamm)*

*Left Bottom: One of Timberline's more recent innovations is Children's Weekend, which features elephant rides from Wildlife Safari and the appearance of a number of creatures from the Washington Park Zoo in Portland. (Photo: Bill White)*

*Above Left: Hot air balloons add excitement to special events held at Timberline. (Photo: Richard Kohnstamm)*

*Above Center: Antique car clubs often meet at Timberline. The approach, which was first made by John B. Kelly in August 1903, has improved since the stalwart Portlander drove his White-Stanhope steamer to Government Camp. (Photo: Warren Olney)*

*Above Right: Many hikers have heard the sound of bag pipes as they walked the last miles back to Timberline Lodge. During the 1960s and 1970s, Highland Weekend flourished at Timberline. (Photo: Ragnars Veilunds)*

59

*The view from Tom Dick Ridge shows a snow-capped Mount Hood. (Photo: John Marshall)*

Another major source of support for Kohnstamm has been his wife Molly. "We have an unconventional family life, that's for sure," says Kohnstamm. "They live in Portland and I'm only in the city two days a week. All four of our sons have worked at the Lodge and one has gone to hotel school and learned the trade. It hasn't been easy for my wife, but we both enjoy the independence life at Timberline has given us. When you are in the hotel business, one of the things you give up is a normal schedule. Part of what it takes to make this place go is a lot of personal attention. It's essential to the ambience here to know that there's someone in charge who cares."

Kohnstamm's next ambition is to assure Timberline's economic self-sufficiency by adding sixty-eight guest rooms. "I'm not sure this will be possible — it's so expensive to build up here — but we're working on it. We're really still in the middle of accomplishing the long-range plan. The permit dispute in the 1970s slowed Timberline's success way down. Now we've finally got some momentum."

No matter how well-conceived or intended his personal vision might be, Kohnstamm has learned that it must conform to the needs and opinions of Timberline's users. "My first real tussle with public opinion showed me this," he says. "Everyone thought of the Lodge's Saint Bernard dogs as the very symbol of Timberline. Actually, the first dogs here were two white Great Pyrenees, but they became hard to find and the Saint Bernards were brought in. I had a publicity guy working for me who loved huskies. He thought Saint Bernards were clumsy and not so sharp, so he brought huskies in to replace them. The public absolutely *rejected* the huskies and *demanded* to have the Saint Bernards back. I discovered the public lets you know exactly what it thinks about changes at Timberline and when you run counter to their views — boy, do they tell you right away. That's one of the main reasons I feel confident about the future of Timberline. I get good reactions from the public. The public in general seems very pleased with the development of Timberline and, needless to say, I am too."

*Above: Since 1937, through sun and gale, Timberline Lodge has sheltered visitors to the mountain. (Photo: Ron Cronin)*

## REFLECTIONS FROM A TIMBERLINE EMPLOYEE

Why do I work at Timberline Lodge? What keeps me coming back to spend so much of my life on a treacherous, marvelous mountainside?

Maybe it is the everchanging, spectacular sunrises and sunsets that thrill my spirit and overwhelm my senses. Maybe it is the endless variety of snowflakes and icicles in winter, the alpine flowers and bird calls in summer that challenge my imagination. They all seem so fragile and tenacious at the same time.

Maybe it is being part of a team that recognizes the magnificent dream that President Franklin Roosevelt and those who built Timberline held. For them, honest labor was a gift aside from the wage it engendered. They saw people working side by side with each other and nature to accomplish what could never have been realized by just a few individuals.

Maybe it is the ingenuity and creativity that was exhibited by the craftspersons who shared the goal of making a comfortable place for themselves and future generations to experience the mountain and its treasures. And maybe it is the quiet feeling I get in my soul when surrounded by such unbounded beauty and dedication to life.

It is all these reasons, experiences, and memories that bind me to Timberline Lodge and Mount Hood.

## NOTES FROM THE DESK OF RLK

I feel I have the best job in the United States, at least for me. It has allowed me to express myself, to work in a beautiful setting; to see little by little how this 1955 white elephant is being turned into the national treasure it was intended to be. Now that the Lodge is celebrating its Fiftieth Anniversary, it is time to take stock.

People have said that creating special events is Timberline's strongest suit. I guess it is. My biggest "high" was putting on the Bluegrass Festival in 1974. Forty thousand people showed up over a four-day period. It was, as they say, a real happening. I will never forget when the State Police walked into my office before the event was scheduled to start and said, "YOU created this thing — YOU run it! If there's trouble, YOU handle it. We're not coming." And they picked up their hats and walked out. Well, there was no trouble at the Lodge. People were too mellow, and the music was too good.

Putting on Highland weekend for years was also special. I was very fond of Newton Muir, who was the guiding light of Clan Macleay for some time. When he passed away, the Clan held a ceremony for him at the Lodge during which a lone piper played a lament from one of our windows. It was a heart-rending experience: the setting, with its wood and stone, the grandeur of the mountains, and the stillness of the summer night with one piper playing.

The celebration of the nation's Bicentennial at Timberline will be remembered through the years. We held a torchlight and fireworks display up on the Palmer snowfield and the crowd loved it. The Bicentennial birthday was the beginning of a new pride in America. I find that people want and need ceremonies and special times in their lives. All of these occasions enhance Timberline, and Timberline enhances them.

I am not a formally religious person, but I am very aware of the spiritual side of life. One cannot live in the mountains and not understand that you do not make a move without the blessing of the Lord or without acknowledging that Nature comes first and that you live on its terms. It keeps you very humble and cautious. Living here also has a calming and strengthening effect on your own being. The very beauty of Mount Hood permeates the way you look at all things.

Part of the fascination of being at Timberline is meeting so many new people — the celebrities, the characters, the phonies, the loves. Timberline employees get caught up with the romantic side of Timberline, and countless couples get married after about a year here. I was no exception.

I came to Mount Hood at age twenty-nine, and it was hard for me to be the boss of people twice my age. But I soon found that most employees want someone else to make decisions for them. Sometimes they know the decision is wrong, but it isn't theirs, so they go along with it. They enjoy watching the boss stub his toe once in awhile. On the other hand, employees do not always realize the energy that responsibility takes. When there is no one else to take the heat, when the buck stops at your desk, you worry about the decision, and sometimes it is years before you learn whether that decision was right. It certainly takes years to arrive at a balance of meaningful employee-management interplay. I have found that fairness is probably the most important management concept.

It has often been said that Timberline belongs on Mount Hood, and that is so true, but it is also true that Timberline fits into the fabric of the Pacific Northwest. It suits its people so well: fine, and very understated; real, and not at all flashy; democratic, and very special. Coming from back East, where things are not the same, I could appreciate all this at a glance. I had always wanted a job that was half outdoors and half indoors and intended to be a camp director when I left college. I wanted to run a place like Timberline, where my efforts would make a difference.

There is only one Timberline, and I am glad I found it.

# A RENAISSANCE

## THE DREAM RENEWED
by Jane Van Cleve

"It takes a special kind of person to make a Timberline *work*," said Dick Buscher of the U.S. Forest Service, recalling vividly those years when the Lodge, like a Phoenix, struggled to shed the ashes of its more troubled past. Buscher knew how many special-permit users dream of making "great little bed-and-breakfast inns" in dilapidated, federally owned structures on intractable, federally owned land in remote, gorgeous settings. And he knew how most dreams "don't include the harsh realities of economics and climate and place — the natural problems that come with anything that's in the outback, the forest, and particularly on a biologic timberline."

But Dick Kohnstamm was different. In 1968, Kohnstamm, a risk-taker and a realist who had good business sense, financial backing, and "enough of a dream" to make it work, projected an agenda that included the renovation of Timberline and the construction of a new wing and a separate day lodge as well as a maintenance building.

To accomplish these objectives, the two men had to surmount the push-pull dynamics between private and public interests while also facing skeptics in both camps who had always distrusted Timberline's viability. When Kohnstamm became the Lodge's area operator in 1955, he found that "Portlanders were beaten by Timberline's continued failure, and nobody quite believed in the potential I could see." Buscher faced a similar resistance. "People with responsibility for recreation in the Forest Service at that time and maybe even today tended to

*Page 64: As part of the Exhibition Center on the ground floor, new tile at the entrance replaced the badly worn concrete floor, enhancing the compass mosaic which was part of the original structure. (Photo: Ron Cronin)*

*Previous Page: Deer newel post (Photo: Ron Cronin)*

*Above: Decades ago, skiers warmed themselves at the fireplace on the ground floor. This is now the location of the Lodge's art and history museum, the Rachael Griffin Historic Exhibition Center. (Viewmaster Ideal Group Inc.)*

resent the Lodge because it was seen as a sort of black hole for all the recreation dollars.''

Even the original builders may have doubted the future of a lodge standing on the side of a major mountain, subject at times to ferocious and unpredictable winter and summer weather. When Buscher and Kohnstamm began to recondition Timberline, they were frustrated and amazed by the discrepancies between the original architectural plans and the built structure.

Buscher told a contractor to expect a three-foot stone masonry wall when routing exhaust pipes out of the building, ''But that wall turned out to be eleven feet thick.'' Dick Hoffmann, the current Forest Service Administrator at Timberline, found a concrete slab laid over the steam system with no access hatches. This kind of ''surprise'' plagued the modern developers with restricted budgets. ''Timberline is a beautiful building to look at, but in the original design,'' says Hoffmann, ''there was no idea of maintaining it. It was as if they built it, put the key in the lock, and walked away.''

But fortunately, something transcendental happens at Timberline. Many of the first workers exceeded their skills to create the mountain temple, and many others would give unstintingly of their time and skill in the future. Lady Bird Johnson, who spent two days at the Lodge in the spring of 1968, touched on Timberline's significance when she told Buscher, ''This Lodge represents the history of the American people and their ability to deal with adversity. It is a magnificent representation of what the artisans and the people of the United States can achieve under a duress situation. That in itself is historic.''

With this historical significance in mind, Kohnstamm and the Forest Service began to refurbish Lodge interiors. They hired well-respected art conservator Jack Lucas to repair damaged paintings and to restore three wood-carved murals, including the rustic *Cougar Resting in Forest* by Florence Thomas. In 1970, the Forest Service commissioned Prison Industries at the U.S. Penitentiary at McNeil Island to construct fifty-two replicas of the Lodge's original dining room chairs. But the managers had meager funds, they were not professional decorators, and when they began to consider commercial furnishings, word leaked out. Dick Buscher received a call from Margery Hoffman Smith, then a successful designer in San Francisco.

Buscher, a big burly outdoorsman, soon found himself perched on a ladder, displaying bolts of fabric for Smith's critical inspection. ''Nothing,'' he says, ''seemed quite right,'' and finally a gracious and determined Mrs. Smith decided to save the old draperies by supervising their re-weaving.

The idea of re-creating the original furnishings obtained further reinforcement from Beth Wright of Seattle, a Lodge guest in 1971, who complained to Kohnstamm about "the shabbiness of her room." After Kohnstamm, who compares the running of Timberline to the running of a battleship, explained some of *his* problems, Mrs. Wright became another "believer."

She volunteered to take her room draperies home, where she conscientiously duplicated both the material and the appliquéd motifs of the originals. More importantly, she advised Kohnstamm to form a non-profit arm of Timberline to undertake a complete and proper restoration of the entire Lodge. In a follow-up letter, which Kohnstamm treasures, Beth Wright gave Kohnstamm a blueprint for the advocacy group which soon would become the Friends of Timberline.

"Everything is timing," Kohnstamm has found. In 1975, the Timberline project seemed to sprout wings. First, the new C.S. Price addition was opened. Then, Kohnstamm was given assurance that funding for a day lodge to reduce the pressures of heavy use on Timberline would be approved. The architectural

*In the first two decades of the Lodge's history, ski traffic did not pose a threat, but by the late 1970s crowds had swollen to four thousand a day. Richard Kohnstamm testified before congressional committees to urge the building of a day lodge. (Photo: Ron McCarl)*

67

firm of Broome, Oringdulph, O'Toole, Rudolph and Associates accepted the commission to begin preliminary designs for the Wy'east Lodge. Finally and serendipitously, Kohnstamm found an organizer for the Friends of Timberline in Jack Mills, a dynamic businessman, skier, and mountain resident, who had just stepped away from his position at the U.S. National Bank where he often worked on Timberline development plans.

Mills believed strongly that the Friends needed clout environmentally and culturally, locally and in Washington, "because we were going to need money and we were going to need a lot of help to do what we wanted to do." He and Kohnstamm invited twenty-five candidates to serve, and twenty-two responded, their names reading like a mini *Who's Who* that included local, state, and national politicians, journalists, photographers, art experts, a representative from the state office of Historical Trusts, members of the mountain community, and distinguished civic leaders. The honorary president was influential Portland businessman Jack Meier, who had played an early, crucial role in developing Timberline Lodge.

Almost immediately, the Friends set three specific objectives: to make an inventory of the Lodge's original furnishings and art objects; to repair or restore those original furnishings still in existence; and to re-create as faithfully as possible those hand-crafted objects that had worn out or disappeared.

The inventory would serve a critical function. By 1975 Timberline was already listed on the National Register of Historic Buildings as an Historic Site and would soon be designated an Historic Landmark. Sarah Munro, with an advanced degree in folklore and previous experience at the Oregon Historical Society, emerged as unofficial archivist and worked with members of the Portland Junior League under the able leadership of Gail Joseph to recover Timberline's "lost" history as accurately as possible. At the same time, Jack Mills had collected $3,000 in initial membership fees from 300 respondents representing thirteen states and two foreign countries. Clearly, the Restoration Campaign had touched a nerve, mobilizing Lodge supporters who also valued Northwest culture and arts.

While Mills worked with Emily Carpenter, Executive Director of the Metropolitan Arts Commission, to successfully apply for CETA support, Rachael Griffin, former curator of the Portland Art Museum, advertised for an appropriate work space in which to restore Timberline textiles. This publicity caught the attention of Marlene Gabel, an artist and teacher, who volunteered a friend's garage. With characteristic resourcefulness, Griffin suggested that Gabel's own studio would be ideal and

*Previous Page: A Lodge guest room warms body and soul with its fire and hand-hooked rug. Volunteers, working since the late 1970s under the direction of Dr. Francis Newton, have made more than one hundred rugs, re-creating original colors and designs. The process of restoration and maintenance is never-ending, and its success is a tribute to Friends of Timberline, who have raised over two million dollars to restore and preserve the Lodge. (Photo: Ron Cronin)*

*Above: On the left, Forest Service Administrator Dick Hoffmann and on the right, staunch Friends of Timberline board member Jack Mills receive the Timberline Lodge award for outstanding service from Dick Kohnstamm. (Photo: Bill White)*

*Right: Dishwashers, by nationally known painter Darrel Austin, was one of the pieces created for the Lodge under the auspices of the Federal Arts Project. Friends of Timberline sponsored the refurbishing of many canvases in the seventies. (Photo: Don Condit)*

Gabel herself would be the perfect director of the highly visible and important textile project.

Gabel began her research in the late summer of 1975, depending heavily on the notebooks and delicate watercolors of Margery Hoffman Smith to determine the materials and the designs used to furnish Timberline's lobby, dining room, mezzanine, and guest rooms. "At the beginning," says Gabel about this gargantuan assignment, "I had no idea how I would get materials. I didn't even know what they were." But she hired three handweavers, including Linda Adamson, who had a good knowledge of dyes and fibers; and seven rug hookers, among them Thelma Dull, a special "expert," who had worked on the original project.

Realizing she faced the same budgetary constraints as Margery Hoffman Smith, Gabel approached the Kandel Knitting Mills for throwaways. "They had tiny, tiny yarn and they gave us boxes and boxes and boxes, but not in one single color." Always resourceful, Gabel borrowed a yarn winder to blend strands of the thin yarn into a variegated, beautifully toned thread for the russets that alternate with bands of cocoa-colored chenille in the Lodge's distinctive, hand-woven draperies. For the appliquéd curtains and bedspreads, she received donations from most of Portland's textile manufacturers, haunted fabric sales, and learned the hard way about variations in quality. At night, she cut out the patterns for leaves, petals, pyramids, and zigzag motifs that Hoffman had favored for her amateur sewers.

Of the original 119 hand-hooked rugs, only eight were still in existence. So Gabel contacted the Rug Hookers Guild for information and obtained generous donations from Pendleton Woolen Mills, which sent truckloads of yardage, most of it in the earth colors that Margery Hoffman Smith had stressed as Northwestern in feeling. For special dyeing, Gabel had acquired an old washing machine and took dyed materials to a big laundromat for drying. When Gabel could not match original color specifications, she would "come close," and the departure was noted on either the Friends of Timberline label or in the very detailed restoration log book. "The artlessness of the original appliquéd curtains and bedspreads were so fitting to those wood-paneled rooms that it became almost sacred to carry on that tradition," affirms Gabel.

The ten textile workers pioneered a commitment that has become a Lodge tradition. By the end of 1978, they had woven 461 yards of material for draperies and upholstery; sewn and lined forty pairs of appliquéd curtains and twenty bedspreads; and hooked eight circular eight-foot rugs, weighing forty pounds

each, for the main lounge; and hooked twenty-eight other rugs.

But a rug in the lobby area lasts just three to five years. When Linny Adamson succeeded Gabel as the textile project coordinator, she and Dr. Francis Newton, former director of the Portland Art Museum and an accomplished rug-hooker, made a successful televised appeal to recruit new volunteers for what is an ever-renewed commitment.

Meanwhile, Ray Neufer, who supervised the original WPA woodworking, found his sturdy and well-constructed tables and chairs required minimal rehabilitation. Arthur McArthur used his own workshop to re-web eleven rawhide-and-iron chairs. Virginia Darcé corrected a clumsy repair job when she restored her glass mosaics for the Blue Ox Bar. And Portland graphic artist Douglas Lynch advised painter Gregory Hessler in the cleaning and refurbishing of the Lynch-designed murals in the original ski grill.

O.B. Dawson's wrought-iron work is nationally celebrated, but the wrought-iron smoking stands were equipped with unique spun-copper ash trays which had, with one exception, disappeared. The survivor served as a model for new copper ash trays, crafted by artisans Dexter Bacon and Carin Mischler. Airline pilot Russell Maugans, a visitor who fell in love with the Lodge's wrought iron, volunteered to re-create twenty-five lampstands in Timberline's signature aesthetic. Maugans was so inspired by Timberline he made blacksmithing his avocation, and studied with O.B. Dawson. Simultaneously, Cecil and Helen Snow replaced the deteriorated shades of guest room lamps with thong-laced parchment identical to the original.

Landscape, *by C.S. Price, the Oregon painter who worked in the early decades of the century. (Photo: Ron Cronin)*

Other treasures — oil paintings and watercolors created by early Northwest artists — were also restored. Two important mural-sized canvases by landscape painter C.S. Price — *Pack Train* and *Huckleberry Pickers* — had been rescued by the Portland Art Museum and were returned to command fresh attention in the C.S. Price convention wing. Paintings by Price, Howard Sewall, Charles Heaney, and Darrel Austin reflected the humanism of the thirties. They were restored and cleaned by Conservator Betty Engel at the Art Museum's Northwest Conservation Laboratory with funding provided by the Friends of Timberline and grants from the National Endowment for the Arts and the Oregon Arts Commission.

With this renewal came new work, including *Mount Hood,* an oil painting by William H. Givler, commissioned by RLK Company; *Grass,* a watercolor by Sally Haley; and *Portrait of C.S. Price* by Portland artist Henk Pander, which was commissioned anonymously through the Friends.

The renaissance called for a Lodge curator, and Linny Adamson, who accepted the position, became a visible symbol of the collaborative vision binding the Forest Service, the RLK Company, and the Friends. Her ten-year commitment to the preservation, conservation, and restoration of Timberline has contributed both continuity and stability to the presence of the Friends on the mountain.

In 1979 the triumvirate met a dramatic new challenge: the construction of the Wy'east Day Lodge. By this time, Kohnstamm, and Dick Hoffmann, representing the Forest Service, had approved the final designs. These were submitted by partner architect Bud Oringdulph and senior designer Richard Spies after a lengthy creative process, which involved consulting architect John Storrs and a design review committee that included architect Pietro Belluschi.

The result was an unobtrusive structure, fabricated in a cement made from crushed mountain stone, with high, almost

*Newly refinished Barlow Room gates at Timberline Lodge have the warm glow that only seasoned lumber can give. (Photo: Ron Cronin)*

73

Moorish arches and distinctive, blunt leading edges. In the winter, Wy'east Lodge is often covered with snow; in the summer, its stony look gives it the effect of a rush of pumice, like other pumice flows on the mountain.

Aesthetic compatibility with the old Lodge was essential. But Kohnstamm and Hoffmann also required a low-maintenance functionality since Wy'east's primary purpose was to relieve Timberline of wear and tear by providing a full array of services to day-users enjoying the mountain. The architects had been charged with accommodating the typical and complex snow-drifting patterns on Mount Hood and with providing a fluid "street system," which allowed people to move freely from a top level with easy access to Timberline to a middle level, where they could eat and relax, to the lower level, where they enter directly from the slopes into a utilitarian compound of shops and service windows.

For the Friends, the architectural harmony between the two lodges was crucial, but they wanted an art connection, too. After Jack Mills had raised $50,000 to commission site-related art works, the Friends set up a committee, and, under the benevolent scrutiny of the Oregon Arts Commission, they attracted submissions from over three hundred Northwest artists. At least two of these artists incorporated references to either the Lodge or its setting in their creative solutions. Bonnie Bronson created an enameled metal frieze at the Wy'east entrance which echoes the strong angles of both the day lodge and the mountain. Fabric artist Dana Boussard superimposed the Indian symbols associated with Margery Hoffman Smith's original design, since her Mount Hood landscape tapestry was a homage to Mrs. Smith, supported in part by a grant from the Hoffman family.

The Wy'east Lodge is also distinguished by its furniture and woodworking, designed and constructed by contemporary Northwest craftspeople. This was a contemporary art investment that the Timberline triumvirate did not expect. Bridget McCarthy, a statewide art consultant and a member of the art committee, voluntarily raised $300,000 so that Wy'east could be a true sequel to Timberline.

Determined that Wy'east be filled with crafted work of the eighties, McCarthy recruited Kohnstamm's help — he allocated $86,000 to the project — and found Jack Mills and the Friends to be willing allies. She was also aided by the example of Margery Hoffman Smith, whom she had known personally and who had been her patron and mentor when McCarthy had served as Executive Director of the Oregon School of Arts and Crafts.

"In the way Margery Hoffman Smith had done the old Lodge, it was not art 'thrown in'; it was art 'thought out,'" McCarthy asserted. "Everything was connected because Margery had understood the relationship of the Lodge to the mountain." McCarthy applied this "local" approach to develop a new funding constituency of skiers, hikers, mountain-climbers, and other Timberline regulars as the backbone of what became a grassroots campaign. Their tribute is the "living art work," *Snowscape*, by Peter Giltner, which features dot-sized portraits of the people who contributed at least ten dollars. Other help came from supporters of specific artists and those individuals or businesses who contributed services and materials.

Critical to the creative process was architect Spies, who volunteered over five hundred hours of his own time, working with artists who were encouraged to use the same materials which distinguished Timberline, but in a current, more technologically sophisticated vernacular. Often the artists collaborated. In his design for the cafeteria furniture, for example, master woodworker Harry Weitzer stipulated wood-topped tables with metal pedestal bases. After ceramists Mick and Barb Lamont had created a clay prototype for these bases, craftsman

*Simple and stately Ponderosa pine pillars support the head house and illustrate the functional form for which Timberline is noted. (Photo: Ron McCarl)*

Vilho Bjorn constructed the wood patterns necessary for the final castings at the Northwest Foundry. Calligrapher Elizabeth Anderson adapted traditional flat-pen letterforms for the spirited "written" signs, the largest cut from steel plating by the Joe Fought Company and the smaller carved in wood by Bill McClelland or silkscreened onto metal by Lee Littlewood.

A certain playfulness, if not outright whimsy, has influenced the democratic array of Wy'east furnishings — even the large cement trash containers designed by Marge Hammond, who collaborated with masons from the Timberlake Job Corps. The furnishings have a sleek casualness that seems appropriate for what Spies has called an "Everyman" building, readily accessible to one million yearly visitors.

Both the restoration of the old Lodge and the development of the Wy'east Lodge expand the tradition that identifies Timberline with Northwest craft arts. To reinforce this association, the Friends of Timberline have sponsored biannual "Mountain High Exhibitions," organized by volunteers like Marilyn Deering, Natalie DeLord, and Harriet "Sis" Hayes, who have been both art lovers and skiers. For one exhibit featuring the metal crafts, the parking lots were peppered with small forges, brought in by the Northwest Blacksmiths Association.

But the parking lots have also been filled with sofa-sized

Saint Bernards for Saint Bernard Weekend and antique cars for Antique Car Weekend. Special events coordinator Bill Conerly even imported an elephant for a special children's event.

Kohnstamm has said that "everybody thinks they own Timberline" — which may explain his policy of keeping the Lodge vital in many different ways and certainly explains the tremendous volunteer contributions which have been made. The RLK Company, the U.S. Forest Service, and the Friends of Timberline are very sensitive to the individual visitor who will associate the Lodge not just with wood, iron, craft, and art, but with unique personal experiences and memories.

Buscher explains, "You get very attached and very protective. I think Timberline got under my skin as a really, really special place." Hoffmann adds, "We don't want Timberline Lodge to be a museum. We want it to be a living, breathing business that happens to be in an historical building." And Dick Kohnstamm says, "My whole philosophy of operating the Lodge is that it should be a celebration of life. I wanted to see Timberline successful, and that's happening. It's taken much longer than I thought it would, but I've also learned that the getting there is half the fun. And it doesn't matter if you don't accomplish your dream right away as long as there is improvement. As long as you can see progress — that keeps you going."

*The Wy'east Day Lodge was built in 1982 to relieve the Lodge of an overburden of skiers. The day lodge has taken the confusion and paper cups out of Timberline Lodge and returned it to the original purpose framed by its private and government builders: a hotel. (Photo: Tony Price)*

# FRIENDS AND LOVERS

## A PERSONAL VIEW
by Jack Mills

Margery Hoffman Smith remembered the tears in the eyes of tough workmen when the Timberline Lodge construction project was completed and the team split up.

Kate McCarthy recalls waiting on tables in the Cascade Dining Room September 28, 1937, just after President Roosevelt's address, her Timberline honeymoon in 1942, and her fortieth anniversary party at the Lodge in 1982.

Joan Mondale wrote of her desire to bring her husband, former Vice-President Fritz Mondale, and her children back to Timberline for a visit. And then there is the famous line from a Boise, Idaho, surgeon: "Timberline Lodge brings to mind memories of some of my fondest indiscretions."

Oregon's favorite structure has touched the personal lives of millions. My life is no exception. My wife, a Timberline skier since high school, insisted I make my first trip to Mount Hood and Timberline in 1951, when I was twenty-one. The real reason for the journey was to watch Jimmy Stewart being filmed in *Bend in the River,* which was shot on the hillside in front of the Lodge. With this as an introduction, I was exposed.

Some fifteen years later, as a commercial loan officer, I became Timberline's banker. This gave me another perspective on the business struggle of a lodge at the six-thousand-foot level on the south slope of Oregon's tallest mountain.

Then, add another ten years, and in 1975 Friends of Timberline began work and my serious love affair with Timberline commenced. Of the four recent decades of my life, I have

enjoyed the last decade most, primarily because of my close association with Timberline Lodge, its people, and the mountain. It did not take long to be caught up by emotions which resembled those the tough workmen experienced in 1937.

True, it is just a building made of wood, stone, metal, and glass, and the same materials may be found in thousands of structures around the world. However, its location and design, the reason for its continued existence, and its designation as a National Historic Landmark make Timberline Lodge more than just another building.

For fifty years, Timberline Lodge has been a significant part of Oregon's history and politics. For half a century, Oregonians have proudly taken their out-of-state relatives and friends to visit their own magnificent mountain lodge. Now, on her golden anniversary, Timberline Lodge is called a "must see" in national publications and international travel brochures, and the United States Postal Service is issuing a commemorative Timberline Lodge postcard on September 28, 1987. That ski lodge on Mount Hood has made it on the world map.

The Timberline story is a love story. I have served on the boards of over forty non-profit organizations in the past twenty years, and in my experience Friends of Timberline is the first and only such group that has proven totally non-controversial. When the public, and the people making up that public, are truly in love, there is no conflict.

Another reason for the Friends' popularity is the consistently high quality and effectiveness of its board members. One member of that board, Dr. J. Gordon Grout, has diligently chaired the nominating committee for years. Patricia Wessinger established the membership program as a charter board member and now, eleven years later, is assisting with the new Timberline landscaping project as a member of the Portland Garden Club and Berry Botanic Garden and Seed Bank. Bob Peirce first brought Friends the coveted Mazamas mailing list and today edits the Friends' newsletter. Dick Balsiger put together the Friends' first serious budgeting process, and Andy Rocchia was instrumental in landing the National Historic Landmark designation. Robertson Collins has been infallible in steering historical funding programs our way, and Dr. Francis Newton, former Director of the Portland Art Museum, has focused his indefatigable energies on preservation.

The Portland Junior League's early involvement gave the Friends an energetic secretary in Carol Zell and, later, a book editor and extremely hard-working board president in Sarah Munro. For that matter, each of the Friends' six board presidents

*Above: Indian motifs have been used in the grillwork that protects windows from heavy snow pressure. Architectural pieces for the massive Lodge were forged in Portland. (Photo: Lawrence Hudetz)*

*Right: One of the delights of growing up in the Pacific Northwest is exploring Timberline as a child. (Photo: David Weintraub)*

has brought personal leadership skills to that important volunteer job. One president, Bill White, not only introduced a needed "hard-nosed" business attitude to the organization but also led the successful five-year crusade for Timberline's recognition by the Postal Service.

Timberline is publicly owned by the U.S. Forest Service under the Department of Agriculture and privately operated by RLK, Incorporated. The Lodge would not be what it is today without the unstinting help of a number of elected officials. U.S. Congressman Wendell Wyatt was instrumental in acquiring federal funding for the new convention wing, which was dedicated in 1975, the year Friends of Timberline began work. Mayor Neil Goldschmidt introduced City of Portland CETA (Comprehensive Employment Training Act) funding to the fabric restoration program eleven years ago. County Commissioners Don Clark and Dennis Buchanan were instrumental in providing additional CETA workers through Multnomah County, an example which was soon followed by Clackamas County. And several years ago, when the National Endowment for the Arts in Washington, D.C., was called regarding a grant application, the distraught voice of an NEA staffer responded, "Yes, we *are* working on your application; your Senator Hatfield has already been rattling our door this morning!"

The political clout of board members serving with Friends has proved essential. However, the sheer drive and insistence on professional quality provided by charter board member and former Portland Art Museum curator Rachael Griffin were instrumental in making Timberline Lodge the world-class institution it is. It was Rachael Griffin's work with co-author Sarah Munro, with funding assistance from the Oregon Arts Commission and the National Endowment for the Arts, that resulted in the outstanding catalog, *Timberline Lodge*. It was Rachael Griffin's dedication that put a curator in Timberline Lodge. It was Rachael Griffin's relentless will that brought to Timberline Lodge a first-class museum, now known as the Rachael Griffin Historic Exhibition Center. By personal example, Rachael Griffin made the board of Friends of Timberline a working board, dedicated to excellence.

The once-damp, black hole of the Lodge's lower level is now the airy Exhibition Center. Here a visitor can stop the clock, for the Center describes the creation of Timberline Lodge and, using modern audio and visual technology, re-creates the Great Depression and the architecture, engineering, and art created in the Northwest during the 1930s. One of the Center's highlights is the life-size replica of the popular Blue Gentian guest room.

*Top: The Rachael Griffin Historic Exhibition Center tells the story of the Lodge's construction and subsequent history. Sponsored by Friends of Timberline, the Center is named after a former Portland Art Museum curator whose energetic spirit helped restore the neglected Lodge to its original glory. The Center was designed by Marge Wintermute with displays by Ken Shores. (Photo: Molly Kohnstamm)*

*Above: Linny Adamson, curator of the Lodge and the Center, has worked since 1975 to preserve a hotel that is also "a living museum." (Photo: Bill White)*

*Right: Timberline Lodge is especially cozy and romantic on a cold winter night. (Photo: John Marshall)*

The viewer looks into this room through an outside window and sees an occupied hotel room in 1937 with period music and the voice of President Franklin Roosevelt coming from the 1930s radio on the bedside table.

Another treasure in the Lodge which has been called a living museum is the Blue Ox Bar. This small operating tavern was restored by the Friends and its original designer, Virginia Darcé, who created the glass mosaics of the legendary Paul Bunyan and his pet blue ox, Babe. Here, the visitor drops back fifty years in time, while enjoying a deli sandwich with beer, wine, sparkling cider, tea, or coffee.

Timberline Lodge is special and will continue to be so.

It is special to the skier because of the beauty of the mountain, its proximity to a major metropolitan area, and the fact that it has the longest ski season on the North American continent.

It is special to the mountain climber as a convenient and welcome point of departure and return when ascending Mount Hood's eleven-thousand-foot summit.

It is special to the hiker as a mail drop on the Pacific Crest Trail and as the start and finish of the forty-mile Timberline Trail, which circles the mountain. (While three or four days are considered normal for this trip, some unusual individuals have run it in six-and-a-half hours.)

It is special to all out-of-doors people who are interested in trees, wild flowers, birds, views, high snow banks, or crisp clean air at six thousand feet above sea level.

It is special to students, historians, architects, engineers, craftspeople, painters, sculptors, and photographers, and all those who delight in the building and its furnishings.

Most important, Timberline is special because it is alone. There is only one Timberline Lodge in the world. I love it because it is itself, as well as a piece of art made up of thousands of pieces of art, one into which I can walk to sit, eat, sleep, and enjoy myself. I suppose this is what we call atmosphere.

Having a love affair with Timberline Lodge has its advantages and disadvantages. One advantage is that the affair does not seem to jeopardize my marriage. The disadvantage is that, being mortal and a few years older than the Lodge, I cannot see this affair continuing much more than another fifty years. By the year 2037, I suspect I will have slowed down a bit, while Timberline will be reaching her prime.

I think of Timberline Lodge at fifty as a beautiful young lady who had a well-publicized birth, followed by a few rough adolescent years. With the introduction of Friends of Timberline, she blossomed into a mature, healthy, attractive, and

Timberline Lodge
Mt. Hood, Oregon

Historic Preservation USA 14

*Page 88-89: Emblazoned against the eastern skies, Mount Hood's sharply carved peak can seem closer to Portland than sixty miles. (Photo: David Weintraub)*

***Top:*** *In an unusual step, Friends of Timberline commissioned Portland painter Henk Pander to paint a Portrait of C.S. Price, the revered Oregon artist who created art for the Lodge. (Photo: Lawrence Hudetz)*

***Above:*** *On Oct. 11, 1986, the U.S. Postal Service honored Timberline Lodge by unveiling this addition to its National Historic Preservation postcard series. The card celebrates the Lodge's Fiftieth Anniversary. (U.S. Postal Service)*

popular young woman with a long and beautiful life before her.

If life for Timberline Lodge begins at fifty, what lies ahead?

Her ski future will be good. The ski industry should grow steadily, although perhaps not as fast as in the boom years of the 1960s. The big ski areas will be getting bigger with their new high-speed, four-seat chairlifts. The little ones may drop out of the picture. Timberline, because of her size and significance, should hold her own in a busy field.

In Timberline's future are plans for a new chairlift to replace Pucci. More overnight facilities will bring the total number of beds to 250, which will match dining room capabilities. An ambitious landscaping project is currently under way to surround the Lodge with the wildflowers that covered those same grounds hundreds of years ago. Seed banks and the skill of some of the Portland Garden Club's wildflower experts will contribute to this difficult endeavor.

While the Lodge enjoys more than one million visitors each year, the sheer number of feet walking around the building makes survival of the fragile plants at 6,000 feet a major problem. The design, funding, and building of paved paths to control the direction of over two million soles will be essential prior to the planting, irrigating, and care of the wildflowers. Like all Timberline projects, this will not be easy, but like those projects it will make Timberline Lodge a showplace and open it to still another worldwide audience.

For its first ten years of operation, Friends of Timberline was governed by the principle that only monies that had been raised would be spent. The board would decide on a project, raise the money to fund it, and then execute that project. As a result, Friends would solicit and spend from $100,000 to $200,000 each year, putting those funds into the hands of Northwest artists and craftspeople.

Now, with a full-time curator and enough finished projects such as the Exhibition Center to require regular income year-round, Friends of Timberline receives two constant sources of income, in addition to special project fundraising. The first is annual membership income. The second is a tax-deductible surcharge on each restored guest room. This revenue is used by the Friends for ongoing operations. These two continuing funding sources bring the non-profit corporation approximately $30,000 each year, which serves as a financial base from which to operate.

The Friends' great responsibility is to guarantee maintenance of the interior art in the Lodge for perpetuity. This, of course, means all the handcrafted furnishings and is a tremendous and

*Above: Wood carving of bull adorns the Lodge. (Photo: Richard Kohnstamm)*

never-ending challenge. Friends will meet this challenge with the help of new board members and new members, with renewed energy and influence.

As a proponent of the pleasures of the flesh and senses these past forty years, I invite the reader to fantasize with me, for a moment. We start the morning at Timberline by riding the Mile and Palmer lifts, while inhaling the cool, clear, non-smells of mountain air, up to an altitude of 8,500 feet. Our bodies warm while skiing down the mountain, looking right to the Coast Range, left to the Great American Desert, and straight ahead, beyond Mount Jefferson and the Cascade mountain range. Without stopping, we ski three miles while dropping thirty-five hundred feet to the five-thousand-foot level, where we catch a chair lift back to Timberline.

When we tire of skiing, we take a dip in the heated, sheltered pool and relax with a cold beer in the famed Blue Ox Bar. After changing clothes in our restored guest room, we listen to soft, live music at the Ram's Head Bar before a gourmet dinner in the Cascade Dining Room. Dinner is superb and is capped with a cordial and more music at the Ram's Head. Back in our room, we enjoy the sight and touch of the handcrafted furnishings, while watching the soft flicker of the fire.

Such is Timberline: today, tomorrow, forever. A love story.

# EXHILARATION

## ON THE MOUNTAIN
### by Tom McAllister

To know the timberline world is to move from winter to summer solstice. Ski in January, when the drifts at the north side of Timberline Lodge are thirty feet high and the trees are snow ghosts encased in diamond frosting. Then hike the slopes in July, when avalanche lilies replace the receding snow bank, and Clark's nutcrackers cry harshly and flash black and white as they fly between islands of whitebark pine in their restless search for ripening cones.

For the high summer experience, take the forty-mile-long Timberline Trail which completely encircles the mountain. This Civilian Conservation Corps project with stone shelters was completed the same summer the Lodge first opened its doors. Marathon hikers have sped through the trail in one day, but to know the mountain is to take three to four days with a backpack. The trail switches down steep-walled canyons pulsing and roaring with glacial-fed streams, traverses parklike stands of mountain hemlock and masses of rhododendron, then climbs upward into alpine glades splashed with the colors of bluebell, aster, lupine, and paintbrush.

Glaciers crouch at the upper edges of these alpine parklands. Hikers leave the trail to climb over heather slopes and sit in the cool breeze that wafts down from a glacier on a hot day. A favorite hike from the Lodge is west 4.7 miles on the trail to Paradise Park. Here marmots whistle their piercing alarms, and black tailed deer in summer red coats browse in the wet meadows on alpine buttercup, marsh marigold, and cinquefoil. As August

*Page 92: Skiers cruise down Palmer snowfield into an evening sunset with the clouds at their feet. (Photo: Larry Schick)*

*Previous Page: Badger newel post (Photo: Ron Cronin)*

*Above: Skiers receive instruction in the "Christiana," a popular turning technique in the 1930s and 1940s. Before the Magic Mile chairlift was constructed in 1939, lessons were held close to the Lodge. (Friends of Timberline)*

*Right: A lone, cross-country skier in the late 1930s wends his way back to the Lodge on a moonlit night. Today, the Pucci chairlift provides illuminated night skiing. (Photo: Ray Atkeson)*

ends, migrating birds follow the crest of the Cascades southward, and in a few hours one can see Cooper's, sharp-shinned, and red-tailed hawks, harriers, and golden eagles riding the thermals as they pass over Paradise Park.

The trail's first thirteen miles, clockwise around the mountain from the Lodge, form part of the 2,400-mile-long Pacific Crest Trail, which runs along the backbone of the Sierra and Cascade ranges from Mexico to Canada. For hikers serious about doing all or a portion of this route, the Lodge is a way station for supply packages and mail and a meeting point with friends and family. Some start, some end, and many pass through the Lodge on their great adventure.

Ski racing entered the Timberline experience and tradition on the same day, June 14, 1936, that the cornerstone was laid. On that occasion, Mazamas Cup racers climbed to the ten-thousand-foot level at Crater Rock for the start of their combined downhill and slalom event. Those early racers were as much mountaineers as skiers. They used sealskin climbers on

*Skiers cavort down Palmer Snowfield with Illumination Rock towering behind. Palmer, which is reached by chair, lies at an elevation of 8,500 feet. (Photo: Mike Epstein)*

**Right:** *After violent storms, Mount Hood often clears to a pristine beauty. A discerning eye will note that three of Palmer's lift towers have toppled. (Photo: Larry Schick)*

their skis to get up the mountain or shouldered their boards and slogged upward to reach the starting gate. Cascade Ski Club members Hjalmar Hvam and Boyd French, Jr. took first and second places in that Timberline race, and Jack Meier was chairman of the event, which was aired over the National Broadcasting Company network by radio station KGW, Portland.

In the ensuing years, four top racing events were held annually at Timberline: the Golden Rose, Portland Day Trail, Golden Poles, and Arnold Lunn races. But it is the Portland Day Trail Race and the Golden Rose Ski Classic which have endured.

The Portland Day Trail Race is a favorite with the local ski community because it celebrates a ski history going back to the 1930s, when a downhill run was earned by climbing above the site of Timberline Lodge and then picking a route which dropped three thousand feet in elevation down to Government Camp, Mazamas Lodge, or Summit Ski Area. There was no lift capacity, aside from a few primitive rope tows.

Always held in early June, the Golden Rose is a Portland Rose Festival event and the only sanctioned summer ski race in the nation. Its timing is ideal because with racers off the regular circuit there are no conflicts, and the presence of the best pro-am

racers in the country, as well as United States and Canadian alpine ski team members, gives the race a high point value. The first Golden Rose slalom race was June 13, 1937, the same day Timberline Lodge held its first open house. Three thousand attended, and Hjalmar Hvam won the race, then jumped off a cornice and broke his leg.

Sir Arnold Lunn, the father of slalom racing (he laid out the first course at Murren, Switzerland, in 1922) and the Britisher who brought recognition to downhill and slalom in the Federation Internationale de Ski (FIS), spoke from the parapet over the Lodge entry when Timberline's first Arnold Lunn downhill event opened on November 21, 1937. Lunn marveled at Timberline's year-round skiing potential, encouraged American skiers to enter world competition, and prophetically noted that a tram up to Crater Rock would bring the mountain to its fullest ski potential.

That first Lunn downhill race had a geschmozzle start — everyone in a bunch with no holds barred for the two-and-a-half miles down to the Lodge. Once again Hjalmar Hvam, a National Class B Four-Event Champion, took the honors.

Kandahar races were the first to feature downhill and slalom

*Page 98: From Reid Glacier, at dawn, the mountain casts a huge and uncanny shadow on the clouds below. (Photo: David Weintraub)*

*Page 99: Pausing for a rest and drinking in the magnificent view of Mount St. Helens before the 1980 eruption, a climber takes a moment to reflect. (Photo: David Weintraub)*

*Pages 100-101: Cross-country skiers climb out of White River Canyon. (Photo: Kent Powloski)*

*Above: Mount Hood is the second most frequently climbed mountain after Fujiyama. (Photo: David Weintraub)*

*Top Right: Snowboarding is a fast-moving and less-expensive approach to winter sports on Mount Hood. (Photo: Charlie Borland)*

*Right Center: Bill Johnson, who trained on Mount Hood as a youngster, returns after his Gold Medal victory at the 1984 Olympics to participate in the Golden Rose ski classic. (Photo: Tony Price)*

*Bottom: Members of the 10th Mountain Infantry Division, which defeated Germany's elite mountain troops in rugged combat during World War II, reunite on the snowfields where some of them skied fifty years ago. Hjalmar Hvam was invited as forerunner. (Photo: David Weintraub)*

racing under international rules. Mount Hood's first Far West Kandahar was inaugurated April 10, 1940, at Timberline and included William Jans and his skiing director, Sigi Engle, from Sun Valley. Nancy Reynolds from Sun Valley, Idaho, and Art Coles of Tyee/Ski Runners Club in Vancouver, B.C., took the combined titles. Maryanne Hill of Government Camp who was racing on the junior circuit was second in both events.

One of the last races before the Lodge shut down for World War II was a January 26, 1942, Interclub Slalom Tournament between Cascade, Timberline, and Multnomah Athletic Club ski teams. The Timberline club won and LaVerne Hughes, Cascade's four-way Northwest junior champion, took best individual honors. Four-way was the tops in those days, for the titleholder truly was the best in downhill, slalom, cross-country, and jumping events.

Some of those young skiers and mountaineers volunteered for the 87th Mountain Infantry Regiment, which trained first at Mount Rainier and formed the nucleus of the famed 10th Mountain Division. Coming full circle, a 10th Mountain reunion race of veterans and their families was held August 10, 1986, on Palmer Snowfield just below Crater Rock, where some of them

raced fifty years ago. Hjalmar Hvam, who first skied Mount Hood in the twenties, was invited and honored as forerunner.

For years, the Blossom, Glade, Alpine, and Cascade trails were the mainstay of the trail skiers, and the Trail Race started at Lone Fir Lookout, with the racers picking the fastest line down, usually Blossom, which had narrow, steep sections between the stumps and trees and washboards and sawtooth turns. Before developments at the Lodge, and as early as the late 1920s, skiers were climbing to the Timberline area and using the old Timberline Cabin to bunk down for the night. The Forest Service built that cabin as an operating base near the head of Sand Canyon. Camp Blossom was a favorite summering spot for campers and climbing parties, and the old Blossom wagon road became a winter ski trail. It was a long way up the mountain from Government Camp with many a break for cheese and schnapps, then a final sigh of relief and one long and glorious if not hair-raising run back to Government Camp.

But of all the old trails down from Timberline Lodge, Glade, which follows in part the route billed as the Ski-way (pronounced sky-way), is the best. For five years, starting in 1951, the Ski-way was the longest and largest aerial tramway in the nation, carrying passengers from a terminal west of Government Camp to a landing one hundred yards west of the Lodge's main entrance. An outpouring of skiers and the need to crack Timberline's traffic and parking problems inspired the formation of the Mount Hood Aerial Transportation Company and the birth of the Ski-way, a project which far exceeded its original cost estimates. (Skiers jumped into the breech by buying $1 shares of Ski-way stock.)

The remarkable Ski-way cars were locally built and operated on the skyhook principle developed by the West Coast logging industry. Riding one was like being in a big metal bus suspended in space, with the cars laboriously pulling themselves up to each of thirty-six towers. The Ski-way died in 1956. Had it used smaller, faster alpine cars on a moving cable instead of a fixed one, the Ski-way might be operating today. Instead, a wide highway replaced the narrow old loop road to Timberline, and parking was expanded.

Glade Trail had volunteer keepers, brothers Lew and Scott Russell, whose winter hobby was operating their own Tucker Sno-Cat on weekends to pack and groom the lower reaches. Accidents on the trail were cut sharply as a result and the brothers were made honorary members of the Mount Hood Ski Patrol. Until 1975, Glade Trail was served by the last of the hand-crank telephones. The U.S. Forest Service, which is

responsible for trails outside the permit ski areas, replaced the hand-crank phones, which were used to report accidents, with an underground cable serving two emergency phones between Timberline and Government Camp.

The Mount Hood Ski Patrol was born out of a need to gather up trail casualties. Formed in 1938, it was the nation's first organized ski patrol. Wy'east Climbers and the Nile River Yacht Club (a group of young Portland businessmen who enjoyed skiing and hiking together) sent Everett Darr and L.B. Barney Macnab to the Forest Service to describe the accident problem and seek help, but they were told there was no budget for patrolling the trails. Then, the Forest Service relented and agreed to pay Hank Lewis, a Wy'easter with a first-aid background, ten dollars per weekend to patrol, using whatever volunteers were available. Macnab ran with the patrol idea, involved both clubs heavily in its formation, and was instrumental in the development of the National Ski Patrol.

The Mount Hood Ski Patrol was a national pacesetter from the outset and currently carries a roster of 300 active members. The first to use Austrian akjas (rescue sleds) in place of toboggans, the first to employ the light and easily laced Johnson splint, designed by patrol chief Harold Johnson, and the first to devise chairlift evacuation harnesses, the patrol was also the first to computerize its accident reports.

By 1941, the patrol was hosting a Northwest Ski Patrol Toboggan Race at Timberline. Teams picked up patients at the top of the Magic Mile lift, treated them for injury and shock, and ran a controlled course to the ski patrol first-aid room next to the Blue Ox Bar in the Lodge. For the sake of public relations, patrollers were admonished to always remove their identification when off-duty in the Blue Ox.

Early Timberline skiers wore wool gabardine pants with a knife crease and the popular Jantzen Knitting Mill reindeer and snowflake pattern sweater. After World War II, and until manufacturers caught up with demand, the khaki marshmallow look dominated and both men and women were clad in baggy mountain trooper pants and parkas.

Gretchen Fraser caused a stir of local pride in 1948 when she became America's first Olympic gold medalist in the special slalom event. Referred to in newspaper accounts as the "pigtailed housewife from Vancouver, Washington," she and her husband, Don Fraser, were frequent Timberline skiers. Don, who won the first Silver Skis Race at Mount Rainier in 1934, was a member of the 1936 United States Olympic Ski Team, and a National Ski Patrol organizer.

*Previous page: Mount Hood offers a range of exhilarating runs to novice and skilled skiers. (Photo: Richard Kohnstamm)*

*Above: Fabulous tanning opportunities fill the long summer afternoons at the pool or on the slopes. (Photo: Jean Arthur)*

*Right: A well-loved hike from the Lodge goes west 4.4 miles on the Timberline Trail to Paradise Park. Almost forty miles of trail were blazed in the mid-1930s by the Civilian Conservation Corps. The Forest Service maintains 150 miles of trails for public use including the Timberline Trail and a portion of the Pacific Crest Trail. (Photo: Charlie Borland)*

The Frasers, who provided the permanent trophy — gold-plated ski poles — for the Golden Poles giant slalom; Barney Macnab of the Mount Hood Ski Patrol; Hjalmar Hvam, legendary jumper and the inventor of the first safety ski binding; and Fred McNeil, who boosted competition and ski area development as an officer of the Cascade Ski Club, the Mazamas, and the Pacific Northwest Ski Association, are the five persons associated with Timberline who have been named to the National Ski Hall of Fame in Ishpeming, Michigan.

Spring was the preferred time for these big races high on the mountain, and the April 29, 1956, Golden Poles race illustrated the mixed moods of the mountain at this altitude. The racers started in brilliant sunshine, but part way down to Silcox Hut they were vexed by enveloping clouds that almost concealed the gates. (Timberline skiers often find they are above the fog or clouds and the mountain seems to float like an island apart.)

Until the development of Timberline, the rope tows operated by the Cascade Ski Club and the Mazamas and the tows at Summit and Ski Bowl provided the only uphill lift capacity. Timberline's original Magic Mile lift was dedicated by Prince, later King, Olaf of Norway in 1939. It was the second chairlift built in the country, following Sun Valley. Alta, Utah, opened a lift in 1938, but it was a converted mine tram, while Timberline's lift, with the first metal towers, was an original. The old Mile lift, which carried 225 passengers an hour, took eleven minutes to reach Silcox Hut and was as much a summer tourist attraction as a ski lift.

By 1940, skiers were pouring up the old Timberline Loop Road to ride the Magic Mile. Today, five double chairlifts spread the skiers over a broad sweep of mountain both above and below the Lodge. Magic Mile and Palmer tap the upper mountain reaches and the permanent snows of summer, while below the Lodge, Pucci, Victoria Station, and Blossom serve the sheltered glades. The well-protected Pucci chairlift is illuminated for night skiing, an exhilarating time for firmer, faster snow conditions and less competition for the runs.

Summer became a nonstop ski season when the Palmer chairlift was dedicated July 4, 1979. The occasion marked the first time in North American ski history that a high-capacity lift accessed a mountain slope with an eternal snowfield. Not that summer skiing and race training were new to Timberline. Beginning in 1956, when Pepi Gable, World Cup champion and Olympic ski team coach from Austria, arrived to head the Timberline Ski School, the Tucker Sno-Cats and a portable Poma lift provided limited summer rides for hundreds where thirty

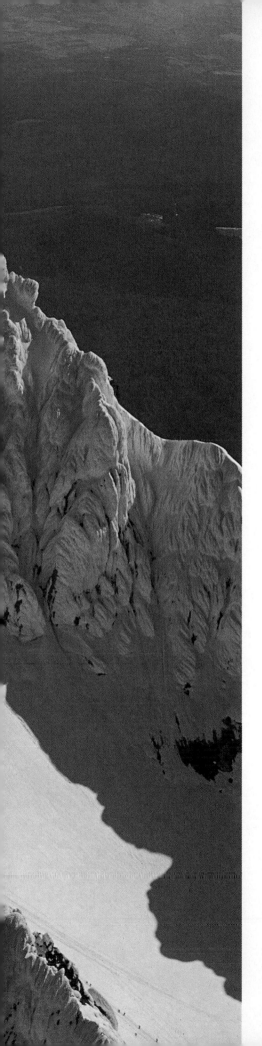

thousand now ski in summer.

The snowfield and the chairlift both bear the name of intrepid Joel Palmer, wagonmaster of an 1845 immigrant train seeking a route to the Willamette Valley around the south side of Mount Hood in an attempt to avoid the perilous journey through the Columbia River Gorge. Palmer, who wore out his moccasins climbing above Mississippi Head to scout the country below, descended by way of the permanent snowfield now famed for summer skiing and race training.

The Palmer chairlift climbs 1,530 vertical feet to debouch at an elevation of 8,500 feet. Steel Cliff, Crater Rock, and the summit crater wall of Mount Hood rear above the lift terminus. Those heights look so bold and close it appears that one could make a dash to the top, but the summit lies almost three thousand vertical feet and a one-and-a-half-mile climb away. From the top of the chairlift, the snowfield falls away wide open, unblemished by rocks or gullies, and the Lodge looks Lilliputian in the far distance.

Most of Palmer, which opened with two hundred skiers weaving downhill in a torchlight parade, is much steeper than Magic Mile, and it is here that the United States and Canadian ski teams have set full-length international slalom and downhill training courses.

Just over a mile in length, Palmer becomes a two-and-a-half-mile run if combined with Magic Mile, where the snow lasts through June. Timberline's winter season now draws 150,000 skiers. It ends in April, when the spring-summer season begins with weekend operation. The summer season goes daily on June 15. After Labor Day, skiing stops for a fall maintenance period and resumes November 15. During ski droughts in other parts of the country, Timberline is a haven for the deprived.

It was Hank Tauber, former U.S. Women's Alpine Team coach and director of Timberline's International Summer Racing School, who convinced Timberline operator Richard Kohnstamm that he could not continue to use Sno-Cats and portable lifts for summer training. The solution was Palmer, which turned out to be the biggest challenge of Kohnstamm's career.

Construction by Riblet Tramway began two years after all the environmental impact studies were completed, and suits in the U.S. District Court and an appeal to the Chief U.S. Forester were dismissed. The original estimate was $565,000 with the Lodge crew doing much of the work, but it took three years and nearly $1 million. Pacific frontal systems, meeting the continent head-on in the heights above Timberline, brought four-foot-thick ice and 140-mile-per-hour winds, which toppled three

110

towers. Working together, Riblet and Kohnstamm redesigned Palmer to a structural standard unmatched by any other lift.

Another skiing first which brought Mount Hood national acclaim was the non-profit ski school that developed in 1947 out of Ski Patrol concerns with a high casualty rate among novice skiers — 97 percent of the cases. The patrol started a Safe Ski School which grew so fast it was picked up by the Portland Jaycees, who raised the support funding and organized and promoted Safe Ski. John Hoefling, who joined the Mount Hood patrol in 1948, was one of those original instructors and is still running one of the three private ski schools operating out of Timberline. Bud Nash, who directed the Jaycees' Safe Ski School, became Timberline's own Ski School Director in 1967 and organized the first National Ski Instructor's Academy.

Safe Ski Schools taught an onrushing generation of new skiers how to fall and get up, the stem, the stem Christiana, the snowplow, cross-country, waxing and equipment care, and never to ski alone. As measured by the declining accident rate, they were a smashing success.

Mount Hood is deeply chiseled by its eleven glaciers. With sea level only twenty-four miles to the north on the Columbia River, and no interposing peaks, the shining mountain dominates and attracts from all sides. Access roads to Timberline on the south, Mount Hood Meadows on the southeast, and Cloud Cap on the northeast help make it the second most frequently climbed glacial peak in the world after Mount Fuji in Japan. As many as 450 people have signed the Forest Service climbing register at Timberline in one day.

Spring is the favored season for climbing, as the snow is still firm. The calmest and most comfortable starting time is the small hours of the morning. Most parties sign the register between midnight and 3 A.M. A few hours later, the black contours of the mountain take bolder form, changing tones from purple to lavender and then pink and gold as the sun washes the night away. The sentinel peaks of the Cascades glow in the new day to north and south, and the wet and dry sides of the state fall away to west and east. Steam wisps floating upward from the fumaroles behind Crater Rock are reminders that the mountain is also a snoozing volcano.

Wy'east Climbers, a close-knit brotherhood of Portland-area hikers and climbers, pioneered many of the most difficult routes with Jim Mount, Everett Darr, Ralph Calkin, Joe Leuthold, and Russ McJury taking the first honors in climbing records. The Wy'easters also pulled off a mountaineering epic whenever the weather and the snow conditions favored them in the spring.

*Pages 108-109: Mountaineers in various parties attempt the final steep slope to the summit of Oregon's highest peak. (Photo: Ray Atkeson)*

*Left: Olympians Steve (left) and Phil Mahre perfect their skills above Timberline on a summer day. (The Oregonian)*

*Above: Without a speck of snow below, a summer skier ascends to Palmer's eternal snowfield. (Photo: Molly Kohnstamm)*

This was the complete one-day ski traverse of Mount Hood first accomplished by Mount and Calkin.

Both climbers and skiers will have an outpost at 7,000 feet when renovation of the rustic stone and timber Silcox Hut, built in the tradition of the hiking huts in the Alps, is completed by a non-profit group, the Friends of Silcox Hut. Constructed in 1939, Silcox was for many years the upper terminus and warming hut for Timberline's original Magic Mile lift.

There is a certain éclat to climbing Mount Hood, but the mountain has a legacy of accidents and deaths, and of valiant rescue efforts. The climbing accident rate is said to be the highest for any peak in the United States. Weather can turn so fast on these lofty heights that a party that started in calm may find itself in the midst of chilling sleet and rain, whiteout and roaring wind, all in a matter of a few hours. This mountain brews its own weather and the climb can turn into a nightmare for those who do not read the signs and obey.

Mount Hood's worst climbing tragedy to date began May 12, 1986, when an Oregon Episcopal School climbing party of thirteen was enveloped in a storm that gripped the mountain for three days. A guide and one student went for help while the two adults and nine students remained at the snow cave, but only two of those found on May 15 after an intensive search survived. Always, the question on Mount Hood is whether to climb or whether to turn back when the weather appears uncertain.

After a number of gallant searches and rescues, various mountaineering, hiking, and skiing groups joined in 1955 to form Mountain Rescue Council of Oregon (MORESCO), which included Wy'east, Mazamas, Crag Rat, Alpinee, Trails Club, and Cascade Ski Club members. The largest training exercise conducted by MORESCO occurred at Timberline in 1961, when four hundred participants from rescue groups all across the country came together. A helicopter demonstration presaged a new dimension in rescue and swift evacuation, and today the 304th Aerospace Rescue and Recovery Squadron of the Air Force Reserve, stationed at Portland's Air National Guard Base, is one of the first on the mountain when assistance is needed.

Timberline, then, is two entities on Mount Hood. It is both a Lodge and a mountain realm where trees surrender to an arctic-alpine environment. Harsh and fragile, the timberline country is a place apart that draws hikers, climbers, downhill and cross-country skiers, photographers, geologists, and naturalists. The historic Lodge is both the focal point and way station for all these interests. It has served as their shelter, their supply and operation base, and their hearth and home in the snow.

*Hundreds joined in the search for missing children and teachers from the Oregon Episcopal School in a desperate effort in May, 1986. The dramatic rescue saved the lives of two children. Mount Hood's danger lies less in the difficulty of its climb than in its extremely variable weather. Deadly storms can sweep in with little notice in a matter of hours. (Photo: Riley Caton)*

*Right: Cross-country skiing is one of the favorite activities on the wooded trails just below Timberline Lodge. One of the Lodge's unique qualities is the lift service just outside the door. (Photo: Kent Powloski)*

*Pages 114-115: At the end of the nineteenth century and the beginning of the twentieth, the north slope of Mount Hood saw the first climbing, snowshoeing, and skiing. (Photo: Bill Hagstotz)*

112

# EPILOGUE

## THE LODESTONE
### by Lute Jerstad

The Fiftieth Anniversary of the dedication of Timberline Lodge is a hallmark. Conceived and constructed during the terrible Depression years, Timberline Lodge is a joyous symbol to those who experience life to its fullest. Over the decades it has served untold millions who came to relax, to celebrate, to meditate, ski, hike, and climb. More than mere brick and mortar, it symbolizes something eternal, a reflection of the mountain on whose flank it is situated.

Mount Hood, which has felt the slats and boots of those who came to experience a different way of life and is the final resting place of some who never returned, may be the most-climbed peak in the world, apart from Mount Fuji in Japan. It has been climbed from all sides, by the blind and physically impaired, by men and women in their seventies and eighties, and by young children. People have skied, bicycled, glissaded, and hang glided over Mount Hood — it is a "non-technical" mountain as mountains go. The skeptic might scoff and ask, "If it's so easy, what's the big deal about Mount Hood?" But ask a thousand people from southwest Washington and northwest Oregon what Mount Hood means to them, and you will hear a thousand different and passionate answers.

Science has answered more questions about "The Mountain" than most of us knew how to ask, or even cared to know. Its pulse has been taken, its heartbeat recorded, its growth rate measured, its tissues and marrow duly analyzed and documented, and even its gastrointestinal system examined. Cartography, vulcanology, glaciology, and geology have explained what it is, how it grew, how it exploded, what makes up its texture, and so forth. That should be the end of it, shouldn't it? Not likely.

What is the ethereal sense one gets from viewing a painting, a sunset, a mountain, an ocean, or even a bird in flight? We know that for some reason such experiences deeply touch the human psyche. They stir some latent, hidden or buried desire in the spirit to seek, to question, and to dream. They add another dimension to the human experience, one which cannot be bought or sold, destroyed or insured, handled or packaged.

To the ancient animists, mountains were the homes of gods or demons, something distinctly supernatural. Greeks, Romans, Afghans, Tibetans, and early European tribes placed the abodes of their ancient gods on high places. Early legends of the Northwest, however, claimed that the mountains themselves were people, with human personalities, under the watchful eye of the Great Spirit, who resided in the sun. Wy'east (Mount Hood) and Pahto (Mount Adams) fought frequent battles, for Pahto was greedy and eager to keep all beaver, bear, deer, elk, berries, and nuts on the north side of the Columbia. Finally, the Great Spirit tired of Pahto's conduct and allowed Wy'east to knock off Pahto's head, thus forming the arêtes on the east side of Mount Adams — the stones are what is left of Pahto's head. Such legends, passed down orally through the ages, reflected the moral codes of ancient peoples.

Modern mankind will claim, of course, that it has risen above superstition and the need to attribute human qualities to natural phenomena. But are we indifferent to the powerful influence these entities exert upon mankind? Interestingly, the purchase of a home in a valley proves far less expensive than the purchase of a similar house on a hill where "one can see the mountains." No pragmatic, logical reason really explains the higher value placed on land within sight of an ocean or mountain. As a society, we endure hardship, spend time and money, and devote a significant amount of mental energy to reach these places. Are there some special, human qualities which inexplicably draw us to these natural wonders?

When one is caught in a severe storm on Mount Hood, one cannot help but recall Wy'east's unleashed fury against Pahto. Sudden gale-force winds, cyclonic conditions, near-instant whiteouts, and blinding snow storms are as severe here as on any mountain in the world. Mount Hood's unpredictable weather has trapped and confused the novice as well as veteran Himalayan climbers. More than a few times this writer has

*Page 116: Wilderness preserves darkness. A time-lapse photograph taken of Mount Hood captures the path of the stars and their distant colors. (Photo: Kent Powloski)*

*Previous Page: Ram's head table leg. (Photo: Tom Iraci)*

*Right: Mount Hood rises quickly from its almost-sea-level base to create a snow-capped contrast with the lush Hood River Valley below. (Photo: Rich Iwasaki)*

118

trudged miles over the Eliot Glacier retrieving equipment strewn about after a tent exploded during the fury of a storm.

In contrast, I have found few days as pleasant as a peaceful siesta on the peak. Perched on the craggy summit rocks, bathed by golden sunshine, I survey the kingdom I left below. One has the rare opportunity to gaze back over the route traveled with perspective. Forgotten are the tired muscles, the aching lungs, the fatigue, the thirst, and perhaps the sunburn. In their place are the awe and wonder of being in the midst of such splendor. The cares of civilization are wafted into space, the tension of human social relationships disappears, and in its place emerges a thrilling sense of peace and tranquility. Those are the moments which bring one back to the mountains. They are the moments in my life which can never be exactly duplicated, and they are also the times which shall never be forgotten.

A mysterious urge brings a portion of mankind to untamed regions of the globe, and an even larger number vicariously revel in what explorers do. The tales of Ernest Shackelton, Robert Peary, Matthew Henson, Charles Lindberg, Captain Cook, Tenzing Norgay, and Edmund Hillary thrill the world. Why? Because they dared to seek the unknown and to roll back the frontiers of fear or ignorance. And because they celebrated what Henrik Ibsen termed the "Joy of Life," that unmitigated, unbounded, raw, lusty pleasure in being alive, and unashamedly relishing every minute of it.

But what is that intangible element which stirs the human soul? And why is it such a pervasive element in so many lives? The answer probably lies partly in escape, partly in dream, partly in questioning the unknown, and partly in a desire to gaze upon natural phenomena for a variety of personal reasons.

Increasingly, the modern world has become both routine and dangerous. While we are bombarded with terror, war, protest, murder, pestilence, as well as natural and man-made disasters, we must fill out forms, pay taxes, drive on the proper side of the highway, park in designated spots, and obey an infinite number of rules. Following the routine, living up to expectations, or simply earning a living can become exceedingly monotonous. Work has its pragmatic role, whether it is carpentry, making shoes, or assembling a drain pipe, and the work-a-day system contributes to human welfare, but it is probably the non-utilitarian endeavors which provide greater meaning and depth. Witnessing a theatrical event, cultivating a beautiful rose garden, viewing a painting, and, yes, gazing at a landscape or mountain — — these require a bit of effort totally divorced from pragmatic function. They are what prompted Robert Service to write:

*The day ends quietly with Mount Hood prominent over Trillium Lake. (Photo: Linda Robinson)*

*Above: The view from the stone balcony of Timberline Lodge on a still summer evening is a memory that many visitors cherish. (Photo: Ragnars Veilands)*

*Right: Mount Hood is a lodestone. It has drawn Indians, explorers, pioneers, and urban dwellers toward its gleaming peak. (Photo: Steve Terrill)*

*Pages 124-125: After a stormy night, with an abundance of new snow weighing down the trees, Timberline Lodge looks forward to a beautiful day on the mountain. (Photo: Ray Atkeson)*

*It's the great, big, broad land 'way up yonder,*
*It's the forests where silence has lease;*
*It's the beauty that thrills me with wonder,*
*It's the stillness that fills me with peace.*

This view, this dream, sparks imagination and seems to resolve conflicts within the self. For some, being in the presence of a natural wonder is a catharsis. For others, it has a calming effect, hones the senses, or purges the self of irrelevant sensations and data. As Kierkegaard wrote, you feel "everything as a whole." You feel "how great and how small" you are.

Mount Hood is a lodestone to those who live within sight of it. It represents something eternal, powerful, mysterious, awe-inspiring, and yes, comforting. Many emotions and questions are evoked merely by gazing at the mountain. "I wonder what goes on up there?" "I wonder how cold it is on the summit today?" "I'm glad I'm not up there in this storm!" Those who climb Mount Hood in some way live out the fantasy, "I wish I could fly like a bird for just one hour and look down at life." They look back at a world momentarily left behind and that view affords a new perspective. Gone are the irrelevant details, the meanness of life, the banalities which block true comprehension.

One of the Indian sages wrote two thousand years ago, "He who merely looketh on the Himalaya, his sins are cleansed." For those who love mountains, and Mount Hood in particular, their love is a way of life. Rejecting boredom, choosing beauty, we discover a dazzling array of stimuli. Such stimulation is easily suppressed in the plains until, "I shall lift up mine eyes unto the hills from whence cometh my help." (Psalms 121:1)

By such experiences, whether viewing the mountain, hiking on its flanks, skiing down its slopes, or climbing it, an indelible impression is etched on the psyche. While driving near it, or simply getting a brief view of it through the clouds, a sudden rush of memories and visions flood the consciousness, and our first utterance may be something as simple as, "There's the mountain." Mount Hood stands like a sentinel, a symbol of eternity and strength, not unlike the mystical Sanskrit syllable *Om,* the beginning and the end, the all-encompassing. When we exclaim, "There's the mountain," all seems well with the world.

The Fiftieth Anniversary of Timberline Lodge, which has nurtured human life on the mountain, is more than the celebration of structures and stones. It is a celebration of life's joy by those who revel in the quest for beauty and who plumb the expanse of the human spirit for meaning. Timberline Lodge is a temple at which life's fullness is shared.

# BIBLIOGRAPHY
## by Sarah Munro

Beckey, Fred. *Mountains of North America: The Great Peaks and Ranges of the Continent.* San Francisco: Sierra Club Books, 1982.

> The chapter on Mount Hood describes the first explorers' accounts of the mountain. Beckey recounts the first ascent (his own) of Yocum Ridge in 1959. Splendid color photographs illustrate the text.

*Builders of Timberline.* U.S. Works Progress Administration, 1937.

> The WPA produced this paperback history of the Lodge in such quantity it can still be purchased at some locations. It is probably the first history after the Lodge was actually completed and is illustrated with black and white lithographic prints designed by some of the artists who produced art for Timberline. Martina Gangle, Virginia Darcé, and Howard Sewall signed some of the illustrations.

Churchill, Clair Warner. *Mt. Hood Timberline Lodge, the realization of a community vision made possible by the Works Progress Administration.* Portland: Metropolitan Press, 1936.

> Only thirty-two copies of this lovely book were printed. Written prior to the decoration of the Lodge, it is illustrated with designs, some of which vary slightly and interestingly from the actual art in the Lodge. Watercolors and drawings of the site and the art are included in color plates. A copy of this rare book is in the John Wilson room at the Multnomah County Library.

Clark, Rosalind. *Oregon Style: Architecture from 1840 to the 1950s.* Portland: Professional Book Center, Inc., 1983.

> The photographs are by Paul Macapia, and editing is by Pamela S. Meidell. Timberline is treated in the section on "Oregon Rustic or National Park Style 1915-1940 " and illustrated by an Oregon Historical Society collection photograph. A one-page description of the building outlines its most significant architectural details and identifies key events in its construction.

*Color Schemes of the Bedrooms at Timberline Lodge.* U.S. Works Progress Administration, circa 1937.

> Completed about 1937, when Timberline Lodge was furnished, this fascinating workbook of watercolors illustrates the designs for the decor of the guest rooms. Coordination of the bedspreads, draperies, upholstery, and rugs is illustrated. The only known copy of this workbook is in the John Wilson room at the Multnomah County Library.

Creese, Walter L. *A Crowning of the American Landscape: Eight Great Spaces and Their Buildings.* Princeton, N.J.: Princeton University Press, 1985.

> Walter Creese is the Chairman of the Department of Architectural History and Preservation within the School of Architecture at the University of Illinois, Urbana campus. Timberline is one of four spaces treated in Part I, "Great Given Spaces." Creese calls Timberline's architecture the "Big Stick Style," an adaptation of the American Stick Style and the English Domestic Style. The chapter on Timberline describes the history of people on Mount Hood, the political background of the Timberline project, the construction and furnishing of the Lodge.

Dodge, Nicholas A. *A Climbing Guide to Oregon.* Beaverton: Touchstone Press, 1975.

> This is a definitive guide to Oregon peaks, including Mount Hood. The routes and the types of ascent are classified, described, and illustrated.

*Furniture Designed and Executed for Timberline Lodge, Mt. Hood National Forest under the direction of Margery Hoffman Smith, Assistant State Director of the Federal Art Project in Oregon, and the general supervision of Gladys M. Everett, State Director of the Division of Women's and Professional Projects.* 2 vols. U.S. Works Progress Administration, 1942.

These two volumes identify all the kinds of furniture designed and built for Timberline Lodge. Each design is illustrated by a photograph and a blueprint. The blueprints were drawn after the furniture was actually constructed because the Project was under pressure to complete the furnishing of the Lodge in time for President Franklin Roosevelt's dedication. Three copies of these volumes are known to have been printed. One set is in the John Wilson room at the Multnomah County Library.

Gano, Ward, and Robert Peirce. "Timberline Lodge—Mt. Hood, Oregon," *Classic Wood Structures.* Forthcoming from American Society of Civil Engineers.

Ward Gano was the regional engineer and, at the time the Lodge was built, the resident engineer on the Timberline project. This article is a structural history of the Lodge and describes Mr. Gano's early experiences on the Timberline project.

Gohs, Carl. *Timberline: a common ground between man and the spirit of the mountain.* Portland: Metropolitan Printing, circa 1972.

This history of the construction of the Lodge includes historical photos and pictures of the art. Photographs illustrate famous people and significant events. A list of contributors to the Lodge is included at the back.

Grauer, Jack. *Mount Hood: A Complete History.* Portland: 1975.

The chapter "Timberline Lodge, Hood's Great Hotel" chronicles the construction of the Lodge. Grauer draws upon newspaper articles beginning in 1935 and ending in 1975, when the book was published.

Griffin, Rachael, and Sarah Munro, eds. *Timberline Lodge.* Portland: Friends of Timberline, 1978.

This catalog contains the only published inventory of furnishings and furniture in Timberline Lodge, three articles about the history, decoration, and restoration of the Lodge, and a chronology of construction kept by the U.S. Forest Service. The second printing includes an updated listing of restored furnishings as of 1980. Black and white photographs include historical shots as well as pictures taken by Lawrence Hudetz for this publication.

Lowe, Don, and Roberta Lowe. *Mt. Hood: Portrait of a Magnificent Mountain.* Caldwell, Ida.: The Caxton Printers, 1975.

This large-format book includes both black and white photographs of the construction of the Lodge and color photographs showing the Lodge at present. The chapter on the Lodge describes its history and operation.

McNeil, Fred H. *Wy'east The Mountain: A Chronicle of Mount Hood.* Portland: The Metropolitan Press, 1937.

Fred McNeil's book went to press soon after President Roosevelt dedicated the Lodge. This "prodigious record" is a compendium of man's associations with the mountain and the geological record. The final chapter describes President Roosevelt's dedication and predicts the new Lodge's dramatic impact.

O'Connor, Francis V., ed. *Art for the Millions: Essays from the 1930s by Artists and Administrators of the WPA Federal Art Project.* Greenwich, Conn.: New York, Graphic Society Ltd., 1973.

A subsection of the chapter "Practical Arts" is called "Arts and Crafts" and includes a reprint of parts of the *Builders of Timberline* by the Federal Arts Project. The essays in this anthology, all written at the time of the Federal Art Project, were compiled as an unpublished report for 1936. Dr. O'Connor located the original manuscript and selected sixty-seven of the essays for this book.

Walton, Elisabeth. "Auto Accommodations." In *Space, Style and Structure: Building in Northwest America,* vol. 2. Edited by Thomas Vaughan and Virginia Guest Ferriday. Portland: Oregon Historical Society, 1974.

> This illustrated article describes Timberline as the "ultimate example of regional mountain architecture" produced during the period between 1915 and 1940. The discussion of construction includes a description of the recommendations of A.D. Taylor, consulting landscape architect. Elisabeth Walton cites the dances performed by the Federal Theatre production to celebrate the opening of the Lodge as an example of collaboration between the arts.

Woolley, Ivan M. *Off to Mount Hood: An Auto Biography of the Old Road.* Portland: Oregon Historical Society, 1959.

> This is a history of the road to Mount Hood and a description of a medical student's experiences driving it in the early years of the century. Many black and white photographs illustrate these memoirs.

## Theses

Cohen, Paul, *Timberline Lodge: Crisis and Contradiction,* B.A. Thesis, Reed College, 1985.

> The thesis developed in this paper is that Timberline Lodge resulted from a social process of stabilization and change. An environment of crisis brought together three unlikely groups: the bourgeois elite, the radical artists and writers on the project, and the Federal Government. These groups saw in Timberline the divergent goals of socialism for the artistic community and rugged individualism and regional culture exemplified by Marjorie Hoffman Smith. Despite varying goals, together these groups produced Timberline: "an ideal blend of business and pleasure." Several articles are forthcoming from this thesis.

Howe, Carolyn, *The Production of Culture on the Oregon Federal Arts Project of the Works Progress Administration,* Master's Thesis, Portland State University, 1980.

> This thesis examines the relationship between art and society, the effect of culture on the Federal Art Project, how the goals of the Federal Art Project were carried out effectively, and the social background of FAP workers. The bibliography identifies individuals who worked on the project, relief and non-relief artists, and craftsworkers.

Weir, Jean B. *Timberline Lodge: A WPA Experiment in Architecture and Crafts,* 2 vols., Ph.D. diss., University of Michigan, 1977.

> Volume I is text and Volume II is all photographs, including a fine photo of Emerson J. Griffith, head of the WPA project in Oregon, which has not appeared elsewhere. This is a comprehensive, historical treatise, detailing the political developments leading to the success of the Timberline project.